The Short Stories of Edith Wharton

Volume VII - Sanctuary & The Bunner Sisters

Edith Newbold Jones was born in New York on January 24, 1862. Born into wealth, this background of privilege gave her a wealth of experience to eventually, after several false starts, produce many works based on it culminating in her Pulitzer Prize winning novel 'The Age Of Innocence'

Marriage to Edward Robbins Wharton, who was 12 years older in 1885 seemed to offer much and for some years they travelled extensively. After some years it was apparent that her husband suffered from acute depression and so the travelling ceased and they retired to The Mount, their estate designed by Edith. By 1908 his condition was said to be incurable and prior to divorcing Edward in 1913 she began an affair, in 1908, with Morton Fullerton, a Times journalist, who was her intellectual equal and allowed her writing talents to push forward and write the novels for which she is so well known.

Acknowledged as one of the great American writers with novels such as Ethan Frome and the House of Mirth among many. Wharton also wrote many short stories, including ghost stories and poems which we are pleased to publish.

Edith Wharton died of a stroke in 1937 at the Domaine Le Pavillon Colombe, her 18th-century house on Rue de Montmorency in Saint-Brice-sous-Forêt.

Index of Contents

SANCTUARY

PART I

I

It is not often that youth allows itself to feel undividedly happy: the sensation is too much the result of selection and elimination to be within reach of the awakening clutch on life. But Kate Orme, for once, had yielded herself to happiness; letting it permeate every faculty as a spring rain soaks into a germinating meadow. There was nothing to account for this sudden sense of beatitude; but was it not this precisely which made it so irresistible, so overwhelming? There had been, within the last two months, since her engagement to Denis Peyton, no distinct addition to the sum of her happiness, and no possibility, she would have affirmed, of adding perceptibly to a total already incalculable. Inwardly and outwardly the conditions of her life were unchanged; but whereas, before, the air had been full of flitting wings, now they seemed to pause over her and she could trust herself to their shelter.

Many influences had combined to build up the centre of brooding peace in which she found herself. Her nature answered to the finest vibrations, and at first her joy in loving had been too great not to bring with it a certain confusion, a readjusting of the whole scenery of life. She found herself in a new country, wherein he who had led her there was least able to be her guide. There were moments when she felt that the first stranger in the street could have interpreted her happiness for her more easily than Denis. Then, as her eye adapted itself, as the lines flowed into each other, opening deep vistas upon new horizons, she began to enter into possession of her kingdom, to entertain the actual sense of its belonging to her. But she had never before felt that she also belonged to it; and this was the feeling which now came to complete her happiness, to give it the hallowing sense of permanence.

She rose from the writing-table where, list in hand, she had been going over the wedding-invitations, and walked toward the drawing-room window. Everything about her seemed to contribute to that rare harmony of feeling which levied a tax on every sense. The large coolness of the room, its fine traditional air of spacious living, its outlook over field and woodland toward the lake lying under the silver bloom of September; the very scent of the late violets in a glass on the writing-table; the rosy-mauve masses of hydrangea in tubs along the terrace; the fall, now and then, of a leaf through the still air—all, somehow, were mingled in the suffusion of well-being that yet made them seem but so much dross upon its current.

The girl's smile prolonged itself at the sight of a figure approaching from the lower slopes above the lake. The path was a short cut from the Peyton place, and she had known that Denis would appear in it at about that hour. Her smile, however, was prolonged not so much by his approach as by her sense of the impossibility of communicating her mood to him. The feeling did not disturb her. She could not imagine sharing her deepest moods with any one, and the world in which she lived with Denis was too bright and spacious to admit of any sense of constraint. Her smile was in truth a tribute to that clear-eyed directness of his which was so often a refuge from her own complexities.

Denis Peyton was used to being met with a smile. He might have been pardoned for thinking smiles the habitual wear of the human countenance; and his estimate of life and of himself was necessarily tinged by the cordial terms on which they had always met each other. He had in fact found life, from the start, an uncommonly agreeable business, culminating fitly enough in his engagement to the only girl he had ever wished to marry, and the inheritance, from his unhappy step-brother, of a fortune which agreeably widened his horizon. Such a combination of circumstances might well justify a young man in thinking himself of some account in the universe; and it seemed the final touch of fitness that the mourning which Denis still wore for poor Arthur should lend a new distinction to his somewhat florid good looks.

Kate Orme was not without an amused perception of her future husband's point of view; but she could enter into it with the tolerance which allows for the inconscient element in all our judgments. There was, for instance, no one more sentimentally humane than Denis's mother, the second Mrs. Peyton, a scented silvery person whose lavender silks and neutral-tinted manner expressed a mind with its blinds drawn down toward all the unpleasantness of life; yet it was clear that Mrs. Peyton saw a "dispensation" in the fact that her step-son had never married, and that his death had enabled Denis, at the right moment, to step gracefully into affluence. Was it not, after all, a sign of healthy-mindedness to take the gifts of the gods in this religious spirit, discovering fresh evidence of "design" in what had once seemed the sad fact of Arthur's inaccessibility to correction? Mrs. Peyton, beautifully conscious of having done her "best" for Arthur, would have thought it unchristian to repine at the providential failure of her efforts. Denis's deductions were, of course, a little less direct than his mother's. He had, besides, been fond of Arthur, and his efforts to keep the poor fellow straight had been less didactic and more spontaneous. Their result read itself, if not in any change in Arthur's character, at least in the revised wording of his will; and Denis's moral sense was pleasantly fortified by the discovery that it very substantially paid to be a good fellow.

The sense of general providentialness on which Mrs. Peyton reposed had in fact been confirmed by events which reduced Denis's mourning to a mere tribute of respect, since it would have been a mockery to deplore the disappearance of any one who had left behind him such an unsavory wake as poor Arthur. Kate did not quite know what had happened: her father was as firmly convinced as Mrs. Peyton that young girls should not be admitted to any open discussion of life. She could only gather, from the silences and evasions amid which she moved, that a woman had turned up, a woman who was of course "dreadful," and whose dreadfulness appeared to include a sort of shadowy claim upon Arthur. But the claim, whatever it was, had been promptly discredited. The whole question had vanished and the woman with it. The blinds were drawn again on the ugly side of things, and life was resumed on the usual assumption that no such side existed. Kate knew only that a darkness had crossed her sky and left it as unclouded as before.

Was it, perhaps, she now asked herself, the very lifting of the cloud, remote, unthreatening as it had been, which gave such new serenity to her heaven? It was horrible to think that one's deepest security was a mere sense of escape, that happiness was no more than a reprieve. The perversity of such ideas was emphasized by Peyton's approach. He had the gift of restoring things to their normal relations, of carrying one over the chasms of life through the closed tunnel of an incurious cheerfulness. All that was restless and questioning in the girl subsided in his presence, and she was content to take her love as a gift of grace, which began just where the office of reason ended. She was more than ever, to-day, in this mood of charmed surrender. More than ever he seemed the keynote of the accord between herself and life, the centre of a delightful complicity in every surrounding circumstance. One could not look at him without seeing that there was always a fair wind in his sails.

It was carrying him toward her, as usual, at a quick confident pace, which nevertheless lagged a little, she noticed, as he emerged from the beech-grove and struck across the lawn. He walked as though he were tired. She had meant to wait for him on the terrace, held in check by her usual inclination to linger on the threshold of her pleasures; but now something drew her toward him, and she went quickly down the steps and across the lawn.

"Denis, you look tired. I was afraid something had happened."

She had slipped her hand through his arm, and as they moved forward she glanced up at him, struck not so much by any new look in his face as by the fact that her approach had made no change in it.

"I am rather tired. Is your father in?"

"Papa?" She looked up in surprise. "He went to town yesterday. Don't you remember?"

"Of course, I'd forgotten. You're alone, then?" She dropped his arm and stood before him. He was very pale now, with the furrowed look of extreme physical weariness.

"Denis, are you ill? Has anything happened?"

He forced a smile. "Yes, but you needn't look so frightened."

She drew a deep breath of reassurance. He was safe, after all! And all else, for a moment, seemed to swing below the rim of her world.

"Your mother—?" she then said, with a fresh start of fear.

"It's not my mother." They had reached the terrace, and he moved toward the house. "Let us go indoors. There's such a beastly glare out here."

He seemed to find relief in the cool obscurity of the drawing-room, where, after the brightness of the afternoon light, their faces were almost indistinguishable to each other. She sat down, and he moved a few paces away. Before the writing-table he paused to look at the neatly sorted heaps of wedding-cards.

"They are to be sent out to-morrow?"

"Yes."

He turned back and stood before her.

"It's about the woman," he began abruptly—"the woman who pretended to be Arthur's wife."

Kate started as at the clutch of an unacknowledged fear.

"She was his wife, then?"

Peyton made an impatient movement of negation. "If she was, why didn't she prove it? She hadn't a shred of evidence. The courts rejected her appeal."

"Well, then—?"

"Well, she's dead." He paused, and the next words came with difficulty. "She and the child."

"The child? There was a child?"

"Yes."

Kate started up and then sank down. These were not things about which young girls were told. The confused sense of horror had been nothing to this first sharp edge of fact.

"And both are dead?"

"Yes."

"How do you know? My father said she had gone away, gone back to the West—"

"So we thought. But this morning we found her."

"Found her?"

He motioned toward the window. "Out there—in the lake."

"Both?"

"Both."

She drooped before him shudderingly, her eyes hidden, as though to exclude the vision. "She had drowned herself?"

"Yes."

"Oh, poor thing, poor thing!"

They paused awhile, the minutes delving an abyss between them till he threw a few irrelevant words across the silence.

"One of the gardeners found them."

"Poor thing!"

"It was sufficiently horrible."

"Horrible, oh!" She had swung round again to her pole. "Poor Denis! You were not there, you didn't have to—?"

"I had to see her." She felt the instant relief in his voice. He could talk now, could distend his nerves in the warm air of her sympathy. "I had to identify her." He rose nervously and began to pace the room. "It's knocked the wind out of me. I—my God! I couldn't foresee it, could I?" He halted before her with outstretched hands of argument. "I did all I could—it's not my fault, is it?"

"Your fault? Denis!"

"She wouldn't take the money—" He broke off, checked by her awakened glance.

"The money? What money?" Her face changed, hardening as his relaxed. "Had you offered her money to give up the case?"

He stared a moment, and then dismissed the implication with a laugh.

"No—no; after the case was decided against her. She seemed hard up, and I sent Hinton to her with a cheque."

"And she refused it?"

"Yes."

"What did she say?"

"Oh, I don't know, the usual thing. That she'd only wanted to prove she was his wife, on the child's account. That she'd never wanted his money. Hinton said she was very quiet, not in the least excited, but she sent back the cheque."

Kate sat motionless, her head bent, her hands clasped about her knees. She no longer looked at Peyton.

"Could there have been a mistake?" she asked slowly.

"A mistake?"

She raised her head now, and fixed her eyes on his, with a strange insistence of observation. "Could they have been married?" "The courts didn't think so."

"Could the courts have been mistaken?"

He started up again, and threw himself into another chair. "Good God, Kate! We gave her every chance to prove her case, why didn't she do it? You don't know what you're talking about, such things are kept from girls. Why, whenever a man of Arthur's kind dies, such, such women turn up. There are lawyers who live on such jobs, ask your father about it. Of course, this woman expected to be bought off—"

"But if she wouldn't take your money?"

"She expected a big sum, I mean, to drop the case. When she found we meant to fight it, she saw the game was up. I suppose it was her last throw, and she was desperate; we don't know how many times she may have been through the same thing before. That kind of woman is always trying to make money out of the heirs of any man who—who has been about with them."

Kate received this in silence. She had a sense of walking along a narrow ledge of consciousness above a sheer hallucinating depth into which she dared not look. But the depth drew her, and she plunged one terrified glance into it.

"But the child—the child was Arthur's?"

Peyton shrugged his shoulders. "There again, how can we tell? Why, I don't suppose the woman herself, I wish to heaven your father were here to explain!"

She rose and crossed over to him, laying her hands on his shoulders with a gesture almost maternal.

"Don't let us talk of it," she said. "You did all you could. Think what a comfort you were to poor Arthur."

He let her hands lie where she had placed them, without response or resistance.

"I tried, I tried hard to keep him straight!"

"We all know that, every one knows it. And we know how grateful he was, what a difference it made to him in the end. It would have been dreadful to think of his dying out there alone."

She drew him down on a sofa and seated herself by his side. A deep lassitude was upon him, and the hand she had possessed herself of lay in her hold inert.

"It was splendid of you to travel day and night as you did. And then that dreadful week before he died! But for you he would have died alone among strangers."

He sat silent, his head dropping forward, his eyes fixed. "Among strangers," he repeated absently. She looked up, as if struck by a sudden thought. "That poor woman, did you ever see her while you were out there?"

He drew his hand away and gathered his brows together as if in an effort of remembrance.

"I saw her, oh, yes, I saw her." He pushed the tumbled hair from his forehead and stood up. "Let us go out," he said. "My head is in a fog. I want to get away from it all."

A wave of compunction drew her to her feet.

"It was my fault! I ought not to have asked so many questions." She turned and rang the bell. "I'll order the ponies, we shall have time for a drive before sunset."

II

With the sunset in their faces they swept through the keen-scented autumn air at the swiftest pace of Kate's ponies. She had given the reins to Peyton, and he had turned the horses' heads away from the lake, rising by woody upland lanes to the high pastures which still held the sunlight. The horses were fresh enough to claim his undivided attention, and he drove in silence, his smooth fair profile turned to his companion, who sat silent also.

Kate Orme was engaged in one of those rapid mental excursions which were forever sweeping her from the straight path of the actual into uncharted regions of conjecture. Her survey of life had always been marked by the tendency to seek out ultimate relations, to extend her researches to the limit of her imaginative experience. But hitherto she had been like some young captive brought up in a windowless palace whose painted walls she takes for the actual world. Now the palace had been shaken to its base, and through a cleft in the walls she looked out upon life. For the first moment all was indistinguishable blackness; then she began to detect vague shapes and confused gestures in the depths. There were people below there, men like Denis, girls like herself, for under the unlikeness she felt the strange affinity, all struggling in that awful coil of moral darkness, with agonized hands reaching up for rescue. Her heart shrank from the horror of it, and then, in a passion of pity, drew back to the edge of the abyss. Suddenly her eyes turned toward Denis. His face was grave, but less disturbed. And men knew about these things! They carried this abyss in their bosoms, and went about smiling, and sat at the feet of innocence. Could it be that Denis—Denis even—Ah, no! She remembered what he had been to poor Arthur; she understood, now, the vague allusions to what he had tried to do for his brother. He had seen Arthur down there, in that coiling blackness, and had leaned over and tried to drag him out. But Arthur was too deep down, and his arms were interlocked with other arms, they had dragged each other deeper, poor souls, like drowning people who fight together in the waves! Kate's visualizing habit gave a hateful precision and persistency to the image she had evoked, she could not rid herself of the vision of anguished shapes striving together in the darkness. The horror of it took her by the throat, she drew a choking breath, and felt the tears on her face.

Peyton turned to her. The horses were climbing a hill, and his attention had strayed from them.

"This has done me good," he began; but as he looked his voice changed. "Kate! What is it? Why are you crying? Oh, for God's sake, don't!" he ended, his hand closing on her wrist.

She steadied herself and raised her eyes to his.

"I—I couldn't help it," she stammered, struggling in the sudden release of her pent compassion. "It seems so awful that we should stand so close to this horror—that it might have been you who—"

"I who—what on earth do you mean?" he broke in stridently.

"Oh, don't you see? I found myself exulting that you and I were so far from it, above it, safe in ourselves and each other, and then the other feeling came, the sense of selfishness, of going by on the other side; and I tried to realize that it might have been you and I who—who were down there in the night and the flood—"

Peyton let the whip fall on the ponies' flanks. "Upon my soul," he said with a laugh, "you must have a nice opinion of both of us."

The words fell chillingly on the blaze of her self-immolation. Would she never learn to remember that Denis was incapable of mounting such hypothetical pyres? He might be as alive as herself to the direct demands of duty, but of its imaginative claims he was robustly unconscious. The thought brought a wholesome reaction of thankfulness.

"Ah, well," she said, the sunset dilating through her tears, "don't you see that I can bear to think such things only because they're impossibilities? It's easy to look over into the depths if one has a rampart to lean on. What I most pity poor Arthur for is that, instead of that woman lying there, so dreadfully dead, there might have been a girl like me, so exquisitely alive because of him; but it seems cruel, doesn't it, to let what he was not add ever so little to the value of what you are? To let him contribute ever so little to my happiness by the difference there is between you?"

She was conscious, as she spoke, of straying again beyond his reach, through intricacies of sensation new even to her exploring susceptibilities. A happy literalness usually enabled him to strike a short cut through such labyrinths, and rejoin her smiling on the other side; but now she became wonderingly aware that he had been caught in the thick of her hypothesis.

"It's the difference that makes you care for me, then?" he broke out, with a kind of violence which seemed to renew his clutch on her wrist.

"The difference?"

He lashed the ponies again, so sharply that a murmur escaped her, and he drew them up, quivering, with an inconsequent "Steady, boys," at which their back-laid ears protested.

"It's because I'm moral and respectable, and all that, that you're fond of me," he went on; "you're—you're simply in love with my virtues. You couldn't imagine caring if I were down there in the ditch, as you say, with Arthur?"

The question fell on a silence which seemed to deepen suddenly within herself. Every thought hung bated on the sense that something was coming: her whole consciousness became a void to receive it.

"Denis!" she cried.

He turned on her almost savagely. "I don't want your pity, you know," he burst out. "You can keep that for Arthur. I had an idea women loved men for themselves, through everything, I mean. But I wouldn't steal your love, I don't want it on false pretenses, you understand. Go and look into other men's lives, that's all I ask of you. I slipped into it, it was just a case of holding my tongue when I ought to have spoken—but I—I—for God's sake, don't sit there staring! I suppose you've seen all along that I knew he was married to the woman."

III

The housekeeper's reminding her that Mr. Orme would be at home the next day for dinner, and did she think he would like the venison with claret sauce or jelly, roused Kate to the first consciousness of her surroundings. Her father would return on the morrow: he would give to the dressing of the venison such minute consideration as, in his opinion, every detail affecting his comfort or convenience quite obviously merited. And if it were not the venison it would be something else; if it were not the housekeeper it would be Mr. Orme, charged with the results of a conference with his agent, a committee-meeting at his club, or any of the other incidents which, by happening to himself, became events. Kate found herself caught in the inexorable continuity of life, found herself gazing over a scene of ruin lit up by the punctual recurrence of habit as nature's calm stare lights the morrow of a whirlwind.

Life was going on, then, and dragging her at its wheels. She could neither check its rush nor wrench loose from it and drop out, oh, how blessedly, into darkness and cessation. She must go bounding on, racked, broken, but alive in every fibre. The most she could hope was a few hours' respite, not from her own terrors, but from the pressure of outward claims: the midday halt, during which the victim is unbound while his torturers rest from their efforts. Till her father's return she would have the house to herself, and, the question of the venison despatched, could give herself to long lonely pacings of the empty rooms, and shuddering subsidences upon her pillow.

Her first impulse, as the mist cleared from her brain, was the habitual one of reaching out for ultimate relations. She wanted to know the worst; and for her, as she saw in a flash, the worst of it was the core of fatality in what had happened. She shrank from her own way of putting it—nor was it even figuratively true that she had ever felt, under faith in Denis, any such doubt as the perception implied. But that was merely because her imagination had never put him to the test. She was fond of exposing herself to hypothetical ordeals, but somehow she had never carried Denis with her on these adventures. What she saw now was that, in a world of strangeness, he remained the object least strange to her. She was not in the tragic case of the girl who suddenly sees her lover unmasked. No mask had dropped from Denis's face: the pink shades had simply been lifted from the lamps, and she saw him for the first time in an unmitigated glare.

Such exposure does not alter the features, but it lays an ugly emphasis on the most charming lines, pushing the smile to a grin, the curve of good-nature to the droop of slackness. And it was precisely into the flagging lines of extreme weakness that Denis's graceful contour flowed. In the terrible talk which had followed his avowal, and wherein every word flashed a light on his moral processes, she had been less startled by what he had done than by the way in which his conscience had already become a passive surface for the channelling of consequences. He was like a child who had put a match to the curtains, and stands agape at the blaze. It was horribly naughty to put the match, but beyond that the child's responsibility did not extend. In this business of Arthur's, where all had been wrong from the beginning—where self-defence might well find a plea for its casuistries in the absence of a definite right to be measured by—it had been easy, after the first slip, to drop a little lower with each struggle. The woman—oh, the woman was—well, of the kind who prey on such men. Arthur, out there, at his lowest ebb, had drifted into living with her as a man drifts into drink or opium. He knew what she was—he knew where she had come from. But he had fallen ill, and she had nursed him—nursed him devotedly, of course. That was her chance, and she knew it. Before he was out of the fever she had the noose around him—he came to and found himself married. Such cases were common enough—if the man recovered he bought off the woman and got a divorce. It was all a part of the business—the marriage, the bribe, the divorce. Some of those women made a big income out of it—they were married and divorced once a year. If Arthur had only got well—but, instead, he had a relapse and died. And there was the woman, made his widow by mischance as it were, with her child on her arm—whose child?—and a scoundrelly black-mailing lawyer to work up her case for her. Her claim was clear enough—the right of dower, a third of his estate. But if he had never meant to marry her? If he had been trapped as patently as a rustic fleeced in a gambling-hell? Arthur, in his last hours, had confessed to the marriage, but had also acknowledged its folly. And after his death, when Denis came to look about him and make inquiries, he found that the witnesses, if there had been any, were dispersed and undiscoverable. The whole question hinged on Arthur's statement to his brother. Suppress that statement, and the claim vanished, and with it the scandal, the humiliation, the life-long burden of the woman and child dragging the name of Peyton through heaven knew what depths. He had thought of that first, Denis swore, rather than of the money. The money, of course, had made a difference, he was too honest not to own it—but not till afterward, he declared—would have declared on his honour, but that the word tripped him up, and sent a flush to his forehead.

Thus, in broken phrases, he flung his defence at her: a defence improvised, pieced together as he went along, to mask the crude instinctiveness of his act. For with increasing clearness Kate saw, as she listened, that there had been no real struggle in his mind; that, but for the grim logic of chance, he might never have felt the need of any justification. If the woman, after the manner of such baffled huntresses, had wandered off in search of fresh prey, he might, quite sincerely, have congratulated himself on having saved a decent name and an honest fortune from her talons. It was the price she had paid to establish her claim that for the first time brought him to a startled sense of its justice. His conscience responded only to the concrete pressure of facts.

It was with the anguish of this discovery that Kate Orme locked herself in at the end of their talk. How the talk had ended, how at length she had got him from the room and the house, she recalled but confusedly. The tragedy of the woman's death, and of his own share in it, were as nothing in the disaster of his bright irreclaimableness. Once, when she had cried out, "You would have married me and said nothing," and he groaned back, "But I have told you," she felt like a trainer with a lash above some bewildered animal.

But she persisted savagely. "You told me because you had to; because your nerves gave way; because you knew it couldn't hurt you to tell." The perplexed appeal of his gaze had almost checked her. "You told me because it was a relief; but nothing will really relieve you—nothing will really help you, till you have told some one who, who will hurt you."

"Who will hurt me—?"

"Till you have told the truth as—as openly as you lied."

He started up, ghastly with fear. "I don't understand you."

"You must confess, then—publicly—openly—you must go to the judge. I don't know how it's done."

"To the judge? When they're both dead? When everything is at an end? What good could that do?" he groaned.

"Everything is not at an end for you—everything is just beginning. You must clear yourself of this guilt; and there is only one way—to confess it. And you must give back the money."

This seemed to strike him as conclusive proof of her irrelevance. "I wish I had never heard of the money! But to whom would you have me give it back? I tell you she was a waif out of the gutter. I don't believe any one knew her real name—I don't believe she had one."

"She must have had a mother and father."

"Am I to devote my life to hunting for them through the slums of California? And how shall I know when I have found them? It's impossible to make you understand. I did wrong, I did horribly wrong, but that is not the way to repair it."

"What is, then?"

He paused, a little askance at the question. "To do better—to do my best," he said, with a sudden flourish of firmness. "To take warning by this dreadful—"

"Oh, be silent," she cried out, and hid her face. He looked at her hopelessly.

At last he said: "I don't know what good it can do to go on talking. I have only one more thing to say. Of course you know that you are free."

He spoke simply, with a sudden return to his old voice and accent, at which she weakened as under a caress. She lifted her head and gazed at him. "Am I?" she said musingly.

"Kate!" burst from him; but she raised a silencing hand.

"It seems to me," she said, "that I am imprisoned, imprisoned with you in this dreadful thing. First I must help you to get out, then it will be time enough to think of myself."

His face fell and he stammered: "I don't understand you."

"I can't say what I shall do, or how I shall feel, till I know what you are going to do and feel."

"You must see how I feel, that I'm half dead with it."

"Yes, but that is only half."

He turned this over for a perceptible space of time before asking slowly: "You mean that you'll give me up, if I don't do this crazy thing you propose?"

She paused in turn. "No," she said; "I don't want to bribe you. You must feel the need of it yourself."

"The need of proclaiming this thing publicly?"

"Yes."

He sat staring before him. "Of course you realize what it would mean?" he began at length.

"To you?" she returned.

"I put that aside. To others—to you. I should go to prison."

"I suppose so," she said simply.

"You seem to take it very easily, I'm afraid my mother wouldn't."

"Your mother?" This produced the effect he had expected.

"You hadn't thought of her, I suppose? It would probably kill her."

"It would have killed her to think that you could do what you have done!"

"It would have made her very unhappy; but there's a difference."

Yes: there was a difference; a difference which no rhetoric could disguise. The secret sin would have made Mrs. Peyton wretched, but it would not have killed her. And she would have taken precisely Denis's view of the elasticity of atonement: she would have accepted private regrets as the genteel equivalent of open expiation. Kate could even imagine her extracting a "lesson" from the providential fact that her son had not been found out.

"You see it's not so simple," he broke out, with a tinge of doleful triumph.

"No: it's not simple," she assented.

"One must think of others," he continued, gathering faith in his argument as he saw her reduced to acquiescence.

She made no answer, and after a moment he rose to go. So far, in retrospect, she could follow the course of their talk; but when, in the act of parting, argument lapsed into entreaty, and renunciation into the passionate appeal to give him at least one more hearing, her memory lost itself in a tumult of pain, and she recalled only that, when the door closed on him, he took with him her promise to see him once again.

IV

She had promised to see him again; but the promise did not imply that she had rejected his offer of freedom. In the first rush of misery she had not fully repossessed herself, had felt herself entangled in his fate by a hundred meshes of association and habit; but after a sleepless night spent with the thought of him, that dreadful bridal of their souls, she woke to a morrow in which he had no part. She had not sought her freedom, nor had he given it; but a chasm had opened at their feet, and they found themselves on different sides.

Now she was able to scan the disaster from the melancholy vantage of her independence. She could even draw a solace from the fact that she had ceased to love Denis. It was inconceivable that an emotion so interwoven with every fibre of consciousness should cease as suddenly as the flow of sap in an uprooted plant; but she had never allowed herself to be tricked by the current phraseology of sentiment, and there were no stock axioms to protect her from the truth.

It was probably because she had ceased to love him that she could look forward with a kind of ghastly composure to seeing him again. She had stipulated, of course, that the wedding should be put off, but she had named no other condition beyond asking for two days to herself, two days during which he was not even to write. She wished to shut herself in with her misery, to accustom herself to it as she had accustomed herself to happiness. But actual seclusion was impossible: the subtle reactions of life almost at once began to break down her defences. She could no more have her wretchedness to herself than any other emotion: all the lives about her were so many unconscious factors in her sensations. She tried to concentrate herself on the thought as to how she could best help poor Denis; for love, in ebbing, had laid bare an unsuspected depth of pity. But she found it more and more difficult to consider his situation in the abstract light of right and wrong. Open expiation still seemed to her the only possible way of healing; but she tried vainly to think of Mrs. Peyton as taking such a view. Yet Mrs. Peyton ought at least to know what had happened: was it not, in the last resort, she who should pronounce on her son's course? For a moment Kate was fascinated by this evasion of responsibility; she had nearly decided to tell Denis that he must begin by confessing everything to his mother. But almost at once she began to shrink from the consequences. There was nothing she so dreaded for him as that any one should take a light view of his act: should turn its irremediableness into an excuse. And this, she foresaw, was what Mrs. Peyton would do. The first burst of misery over, she would envelop the whole situation in a mist of expediency. Brought to the bar of Kate's judgment, she at once revealed herself incapable of higher action.

Kate's conception of her was still under arraignment when the actual Mrs. Peyton fluttered in. It was the afternoon of the second day, as the girl phrased it in the dismal re-creation of her universe. She had been thinking so hard of Mrs. Peyton that the lady's silvery insubstantial presence seemed hardly more than a projection of the thought; but as Kate collected herself, and regained contact with the outer world, her preoccupation yielded to surprise. It was unusual for Mrs. Peyton to pay visits. For years she had remained enthroned in a semi-invalidism which prohibited effort while it did not preclude diversion; and the girl at once divined a special purpose in her coming.

Mrs. Peyton's traditions would not have permitted any direct method of attack; and Kate had to sit through the usual prelude of ejaculation and anecdote. Presently, however, the elder lady's voice gathered significance, and laying her hand on Kate's she murmured: "I have come to talk to you of this sad affair."

Kate began to tremble. Was it possible that Denis had after all spoken? A rising hope checked her utterance, and she saw in a flash that it still lay with him to regain his hold on her. But Mrs. Peyton went on delicately: "It has been a great shock to my poor boy. To be brought in contact with Arthur's past was in itself inexpressibly painful; but this last dreadful business, that woman's wicked act—"

"Wicked?" Kate exclaimed.

Mrs. Peyton's gentle stare reproved her. "Surely religion teaches us that suicide is a sin? And to murder her child! I ought not to speak to you of such things, my dear. No one has ever mentioned anything so dreadful in my presence: my dear husband used to screen me so carefully from the painful side of life. Where there is so much that is beautiful to dwell upon, we should try to ignore the existence of such horrors. But nowadays everything is in the papers; and Denis told me he thought it better that you should hear the news first from him."

Kate nodded without speaking.

"He felt how dreadful it was to have to tell you. But I tell him he takes a morbid view of the case. Of course one is shocked at the woman's crime, but, if one looks a little deeper, how can one help seeing that it may have been designed as the means of rescuing that poor child from a life of vice and misery? That is the view I want Denis to take: I want him to see how all the difficulties of life disappear when one has learned to look for a divine purpose in human sufferings."

Mrs. Peyton rested a moment on this period, as an experienced climber pauses to be overtaken by a less agile companion; but presently she became aware that Kate was still far below her, and perhaps needed a stronger incentive to the ascent.

"My dear child," she said adroitly, "I said just now that I was sorry you had been obliged to hear of this sad affair; but after all it is only you who can avert its consequences."

Kate drew an eager breath. "Its consequences?" she faltered.

Mrs. Peyton's voice dropped solemnly. "Denis has told me everything," she said.

"Everything?"

"That you insist on putting off the marriage. Oh, my dear, I do implore you to reconsider that!"

Kate sank back with the sense of having passed again into a region of leaden shadow. "Is that all he told you?"

Mrs. Peyton gazed at her with arch raillery. "All? Isn't it everything—to him?"

"Did he give you my reason, I mean?"

"He said you felt that, after this shocking tragedy, there ought, in decency, to be a delay; and I quite understand the feeling. It does seem too unfortunate that the woman should have chosen this particular time! But you will find as you grow older that life is full of such sad contrasts."

Kate felt herself slowly petrifying under the warm drip of Mrs. Peyton's platitudes.

"It seems to me," the elder lady continued, "that there is only one point from which we ought to consider the question, and that is, its effect on Denis. But for that we ought to refuse to know anything about it. But it has made my boy so unhappy. The law-suit was a cruel ordeal to him—the dreadful notoriety, the revelation of poor Arthur's infirmities. Denis is as sensitive as a woman; it is his unusual refinement of feeling that makes him so worthy of being loved by you. But such sensitiveness may be carried to excess. He ought not to let this unhappy incident prey on him: it shows a lack of trust in the divine ordering of things. That is what troubles me: his faith in life has been shaken. And, you must forgive me, dear child, you will forgive me, I know, but I can't help blaming you a little—"

Mrs. Peyton's accent converted the accusation into a caress, which prolonged itself in a tremulous pressure of Kate's hand.

The girl gazed at her blankly. "You blame me—?"

"Don't be offended, my child. I only fear that your excessive sympathy with Denis, your own delicacy of feeling, may have led you to encourage his morbid ideas. He tells me you were very much shocked, as you naturally would be, as any girl must be, I would not have you otherwise, dear Kate! It is beautiful that you should both feel so; most beautiful; but you know religion teaches us not to yield too much to our grief. Let the dead bury their dead; the living owe themselves to each other. And what had this wretched woman to do with either of you? It is a misfortune for Denis to have been connected in any way with a man of Arthur Peyton's character; but after all, poor Arthur did all he could to atone for the disgrace he brought on us, by making Denis his heir, and I am sure I have no wish to question the decrees of Providence." Mrs. Peyton paused again, and then softly absorbed both of Kate's hands. "For my part," she continued, "I see in it another instance of the beautiful ordering of events. Just after dear Denis's inheritance has removed the last obstacle to your marriage, this sad incident comes to show how desperately he needs you, how cruel it would be to ask him to defer his happiness."

She broke off, shaken out of her habitual placidity by the abrupt withdrawal of the girl's hands. Kate sat inertly staring, but no answer rose to her lips.

At length Mrs. Peyton resumed, gathering her draperies about her with a tentative hint of leave-taking: "I may go home and tell him that you will not put off the wedding?"

Kate was still silent, and her visitor looked at her with the mild surprise of an advocate unaccustomed to plead in vain.

"If your silence means refusal, my dear, I think you ought to realize the responsibility you assume." Mrs. Peyton's voice had acquired an edge of righteous asperity. "If Denis has a fault it is that he is too gentle, too yielding, too readily influenced by those he cares for. Your influence is paramount with him now, but if you turn from him just when he needs your help, who can say what the result will be?"

The argument, though impressively delivered, was hardly of a nature to carry conviction to its hearer; but it was perhaps for that very reason that she suddenly and unexpectedly replied to it by sinking back into her seat with a burst of tears. To Mrs. Peyton, however, tears were the signal of surrender, and, at Kate's side in an instant she hastened to temper her triumph with magnanimity.

"Don't think I don't feel with you; but we must both forget ourselves for our boy's sake. I told him I should come back with your promise."

The arm she had slipped about Kate's shoulder fell back with the girl's start. Kate had seen in a flash what capital would be made of her emotion.

"No, no, you misunderstand me. I can make no promise," she declared.

The older lady sat a moment irresolute; then she restored her arm to the shoulder from which it had been so abruptly displaced.

"My dear child," she said, in a tone of tender confidence, "if I have misunderstood you, ought you not to enlighten me? You asked me just now if Denis had given me your reason for this strange postponement. He gave me one reason, but it seems hardly sufficient to explain your conduct. If there is any other, and I know you well enough to feel sure there is, will you not trust me with it? If my boy has been unhappy enough to displease you, will you not give his mother the chance to plead his cause? Remember, no one should be condemned unheard. As Denis's mother, I have the right to ask for your reason."

"My reason? My reason?" Kate stammered, panting with the exhaustion of the struggle. Oh, if only Mrs. Peyton would release her! "If you have the right to know it, why doesn't he tell you?" she cried.

Mrs. Peyton stood up, quivering. "I will go home and ask him," she said. "I will tell him he had your permission to speak."

She moved toward the door, with the nervous haste of a person unaccustomed to decisive action. But Kate sprang before her.

"No, no; don't ask him! I implore you not to ask him," she cried.

Mrs. Peyton turned on her with sudden authority of voice and gesture. "Do I understand you?" she said. "You admit that you have a reason for putting off your marriage, and yet you forbid me—me, Denis's mother, to ask him what it is? My poor child, I needn't ask, for I know already. If he has offended you, and you refuse him the chance to defend himself, I needn't look farther for your reason: it is simply that you have ceased to love him."

Kate fell back from the door which she had instinctively barricaded.

"Perhaps that is it," she murmured, letting Mrs. Peyton pass.

Mr. Orme's returning carriage-wheels crossed Mrs. Peyton's indignant flight; and an hour later Kate, in the bland candle-light of the dinner-hour, sat listening with practised fortitude to her father's comments on the venison.

She had wondered, as she awaited him in the drawing-room, if he would notice any change in her appearance. It seemed to her that the flagellation of her thoughts must have left visible traces. But Mr. Orme was not a man of subtle perceptions, save where his personal comfort was affected: though his egoism was clothed in the finest feelers, he did not suspect a similar surface in others. His daughter, as part of himself, came within the normal range of his solicitude; but she was an outlying region, a subject province; and Mr. Orme's was a highly centralized polity.

News of the painful incident, he often used Mrs. Peyton's vocabulary, had reached him at his club, and to some extent disturbed the assimilation of a carefully ordered breakfast; but since then two days had passed, and it did not take Mr. Orme forty-eight hours to resign himself to the misfortunes of others. It was all very nasty, of course, and he wished to heaven it hadn't happened to any one about to be connected with him; but he viewed it with the transient annoyance of a gentleman who has been splashed by the mud of a fatal runaway.

Mr. Orme affected, under such circumstances, a bluff and hearty stoicism as remote as possible from Mrs. Peyton's deprecating evasion of facts. It was a bad business; he was sorry Kate should have been mixed up with it; but she would be married soon now, and then she would see that life wasn't exactly a Sunday-school story. Everybody was exposed to such disagreeable accidents: he remembered a case in their own family, oh, a distant cousin whom Kate wouldn't have heard of, a poor fellow who had got entangled with just such a woman, and having (most properly) been sent packing by his father, had justified the latter's course by promptly forging his name, a very nasty affair altogether; but luckily the scandal had been hushed up, the woman bought off, and the prodigal, after a season of probation, safely married to a nice girl with a good income, who was told by the family that the doctors recommended his settling in California.

Luckily the scandal was hushed up: the phrase blazed out against the dark background of Kate's misery. That was doubtless what most people felt, the words represented the consensus of respectable opinion. The best way of repairing a fault was to hide it: to tear up the floor and bury the victim at night. Above all, no coroner and no autopsy!

She began to feel a strange interest in her distant cousin. "And his wife, did she know what he had done?"

Mr. Orme stared. His moral pointed, he had returned to the contemplation of his own affairs.

"His wife? Oh, of course not. The secret has been most admirably kept; but her property was put in trust, so she's quite safe with him."

Her property! Kate wondered if her faith in her husband had also been put in trust, if her sensibilities had been protected from his possible inroads.

"Do you think it quite fair to have deceived her in that way?"

Mr. Orme gave her a puzzled glance: he had no taste for the by-paths of ethical conjecture.

"His people wanted to give the poor fellow another chance; they did the best they could for him."

"And—he has done nothing dishonourable since?"

"Not that I know of: the last I heard was that they had a little boy, and that he was quite happy. At that distance he's not likely to bother us, at all events."

Long after Mr. Orme had left the topic, Kate remained lost in its contemplation. She had begun to perceive that the fair surface of life was honeycombed by a vast system of moral sewage. Every respectable household had its special arrangements for the private disposal of family scandals; it was only among the reckless and improvident that such hygienic precautions were neglected. Who was she to pass judgment on the merits of such a system? The social health must be preserved: the means devised were the result of long experience and the collective instinct of self-preservation. She had meant to tell her father that evening that her marriage had been put off; but she now abstained from doing so, not from any doubt of Mr. Orme's acquiescence, he could always be made to feel the force of conventional scruples, but because the whole question sank into insignificance beside the larger issue which his words had raised.

In her own room, that night, she passed through that travail of the soul of which the deeper life is born. Her first sense was of a great moral loneliness, an isolation more complete, more impenetrable, than that in which the discovery of Denis's act had plunged her. For she had vaguely leaned, then, on a collective sense of justice that should respond to her own ideas of right and wrong: she still believed in the logical correspondence of theory and practice. Now she saw that, among those nearest her, there was no one who recognized the moral need of expiation. She saw that to take her father or Mrs. Peyton into her confidence would be but to widen the circle of sterile misery in which she and Denis moved. At first the aspect of life thus revealed to her seemed simply mean and base, a world where honour was a pact of silence between adroit accomplices. The network of circumstance had tightened round her, and every effort to escape drew its meshes closer. But as her struggles subsided she felt the spiritual release which comes with acceptance: not connivance in dishonour, but recognition of evil. Out of that dark vision light was to come, the shaft of cloud turning to the pillar of fire. For here, at last, life lay before her as it was: not brave, garlanded and victorious, but naked, grovelling and diseased, dragging its maimed limbs through the mud, yet lifting piteous hands to the stars. Love itself, once throned aloft on an altar of dreams, how it stole to her now, storm-beaten and scarred, pleading for the shelter of her breast! Love, indeed, not in the old sense in which she had conceived it, but a graver, austerer presence, the charity of the mystic three. She thought she had ceased to love Denis—but what had she loved in him but her happiness and his? Their affection had been the garden enclosed of the Canticles, where they were to walk forever in a delicate isolation of bliss. But now love appeared to her as something more than this, something wider, deeper, more enduring than the selfish passion of a man and a woman. She saw it in all its far-reaching issues, till the first meeting of two pairs of young eyes kindled a light which might be a high-lifted beacon across dark waters of humanity.

All this did not come to her clearly, consecutively, but in a series of blurred and shifting images. Marriage had meant to her, as it means to girls brought up in ignorance of life, simply the exquisite prolongation of wooing. If she had looked beyond, to the vision of wider ties, it was as a traveller gazes over a land veiled in golden haze, and so far distant that the imagination delays to explore it. But now through the blur of sensations one image strangely persisted, the image of Denis's child. Had she ever before thought of their having a child? She could not remember. She was like one who wakens from a long fever: she recalled nothing of her former self or of her former feelings. She knew only that the vision persisted, the vision of the child whose mother she was not to be. It was impossible that she should marry Denis, her inmost soul rejected him ... but it was just because she was not to be the child's mother that its image followed her so pleadingly. For she saw with perfect clearness the inevitable course of events. Denis would marry some one else, he was one of the men who are fated to marry, and she needed not his mother's reminder that her abandonment of him at an emotional crisis would fling him upon the first sympathy within reach. He would marry a girl who knew nothing of his secret, for Kate was intensely aware that he would never again willingly confess himself, he would marry a girl who trusted him and leaned on him, as she, Kate Orme, the earlier Kate Orme, had done but two days since! And with this deception between them their child would be born: born to an inheritance of secret weakness, a vice of the moral fibre, as it might be born with some hidden physical taint which would destroy it before the cause should be detected.... Well, and what of it? Was she to hold herself responsible? Were not thousands of children born with some such unsuspected taint?... Ah, but if here was one that she could save? What if she, who had had so exquisite a vision of wifehood, should reconstruct from its ruins this vision of protecting maternity, if her love for her lover should be, not lost, but transformed, enlarged, into this passion of charity for his race? If she might expiate and redeem his fault by becoming a refuge from its consequences? Before this strange extension of her love all the old limitations seemed to fall. Something had cleft the surface of self, and there welled up the mysterious primal influences, the sacrificial instinct of her sex, a passion of spiritual motherhood that made her long to fling herself between the unborn child and its fate....

She never knew, then or after, how she reached this mystic climax of effacement; she was only conscious, through her anguish, of that lift of the heart which made one of the saints declare that joy was the inmost core of sorrow. For it was indeed a kind of joy she felt, if old names must serve for such new meanings; a surge of liberating faith in life, the old credo quia absurdum which is the secret cry of all supreme endeavour.

PART II

I

"Does it look nice, mother?"

Dick Peyton met her with the question on the threshold, drawing her gaily into the little square room, and adding, with a laugh with a blush in it: "You know she's an uncommonly noticing person, and little things tell with her."

He swung round on his heel to follow his mother's smiling inspection of the apartment.

"She seems to have all the qualities," Mrs. Denis Peyton remarked, as her circuit finally brought her to the prettily appointed tea-table.

"All," he declared, taking the sting from her emphasis by his prompt adoption of it. Dick had always had a wholesome way of thus appropriating to his own use such small shafts of maternal irony as were now and then aimed at him.

Kate Peyton laughed and loosened her furs. "It looks charmingly," she pronounced, ending her survey by an approach to the window, which gave, far below, the oblique perspective of a long side-street leading to Fifth Avenue.

The high-perched room was Dick Peyton's private office, a retreat partitioned off from the larger enclosure in which, under a north light and on a range of deal tables, three or four young draughtsmen were busily engaged in elaborating his architectural projects. The outer door of the office bore the sign: Peyton and Gill, Architects; but Gill was an utilitarian person, as unobtrusive as his name, who contented himself with a desk in the workroom, and left Dick to lord it alone in the small apartment to which clients were introduced, and where the social part of the business was carried on.

It was to serve, on this occasion, as the scene of a tea designed, as Kate Peyton was vividly aware, to introduce a certain young lady to the scene of her son's labours. Mrs. Peyton had been hearing a great deal lately about Clemence Verney. Dick was naturally expansive, and his close intimacy with his mother, an intimacy fostered by his father's early death, if it had suffered some natural impairment in his school and college days, had of late been revived by four years of comradeship in Paris, where Mrs. Peyton, in a tiny apartment of the Rue de Varennes, had kept house for him during his course of studies at the Beaux Arts. There were indeed not lacking critics of her own sex who accused Kate Peyton of having figured too largely in her son's life; of having failed to efface herself at a period when it is agreed that young men are best left free to try conclusions with the world. Mrs. Peyton, had she cared to defend herself, might have said that Dick, if communicative, was not impressionable, and that the closeness of texture which enabled him to throw off her sarcasms preserved him also from the infiltration of her prejudices. He was certainly no knight of the apron-string, but a seemingly resolute and self-sufficient young man, whose romantic friendship with his mother had merely served to throw a veil of suavity over the hard angles of youth.

But Mrs. Peyton's real excuse was after all one which she would never have given. It was because her intimacy with her son was the one need of her life that she had, with infinite tact and discretion, but with equal persistency, clung to every step of his growth, dissembling herself, adapting herself, rejuvenating herself in the passionate effort to be always within reach, but never in the way.

Denis Peyton had died after seven years of marriage, when his boy was barely six. During those seven years he had managed to squander the best part of the fortune he had inherited from his step-brother; so that, at his death, his widow and son were left with a scant competence. Mrs. Peyton, during her husband's life, had apparently made no effort to restrain his expenditure. She had even been accused by those judicious persons who are always ready with an estimate of their neighbours' motives, of having encouraged poor Denis's improvidence for the gratification of her own ambition. She had in fact, in the early days of their marriage, tried to launch him in politics, and had perhaps drawn somewhat heavily on his funds in the first heat of the contest; but the experiment ending in failure, as Denis Peyton's experiments were apt to end, she had made no farther demands on his exchequer. Her personal tastes were in fact unusually simple, but her outspoken indifference to money was not, in the opinion of her critics, designed to act as a check upon her husband; and it resulted in leaving her, at his death, in straits from which it was impossible not to deduce a moral.

Her small means, and the care of the boy's education, served the widow as a pretext for secluding herself in a socially remote suburb, where it was inferred that she was expiating, on queer food and in ready-made boots, her rash defiance of fortune. Whether or not Mrs. Peyton's penance took this form, she hoarded her substance to such good purpose that she was not only able to give Dick the best of schooling, but to propose, on his leaving Harvard, that he should prolong his studies by another four years at the Beaux Arts. It had been the joy of her life that her boy had early shown a marked bent for a special line of work. She could not have borne to see him reduced to a mere money-getter, yet she was not sorry that their small means forbade the cultivation of an ornamental leisure. In his college days Dick had troubled her by a superabundance of tastes, a restless flitting from one form of artistic expression to another. Whatever art he enjoyed he wished to practise, and he passed from music to painting, from painting to architecture, with an ease which seemed to his mother to indicate lack of purpose rather than excess of talent. She had observed that these changes were usually due, not to self-criticism, but to some external discouragement. Any depreciation of his work was enough to convince him of the uselessness of pursuing that special form of art, and the reaction produced the immediate conviction that he was really destined to shine in some other line of work. He had thus swung from one calling to another till, at the end of his college career, his mother took the decisive step of transplanting him to the Beaux Arts, in the hope that a definite course of study, combined with the stimulus of competition, might fix his wavering aptitudes. The result justified her expectation, and their four years in the Rue de Varennes yielded the happiest confirmation of her belief in him. Dick's ability was recognized not only by his mother, but by his professors. He was engrossed in his work, and his first successes developed his capacity for application. His mother's only fear was that praise was still too necessary to him. She was uncertain how long his ambition would sustain him in the face of failure. He gave lavishly where he was sure of a return; but it remained to be seen if he were capable of production without recognition. She had brought him up in a wholesome scorn of material rewards, and nature seemed, in this direction, to have seconded her training. He was genuinely indifferent to money, and his enjoyment of beauty was of that happy sort which does not generate the wish for possession. As long as the inner eye had food for contemplation, he cared very little for the deficiencies in his surroundings; or, it might rather be said, he felt, in the sum-total of beauty about him, an ownership of appreciation that left him free from the fret of personal desire. Mrs. Peyton had cultivated to excess this disregard of material conditions; but she now began to ask herself whether, in so doing, she had not laid too great a strain on a temperament naturally exalted. In guarding against other tendencies she had perhaps fostered in him too exclusively those qualities which circumstances had brought to an unusual development in herself. His enthusiasms and his disdains were alike too unqualified for that happy mean of character which is the best defence against the surprises of fortune. If she had taught him to set an exaggerated value on ideal rewards, was not that but a shifting of the danger-point on which her fears had always hung? She trembled sometimes to think how little love and a lifelong vigilance had availed in the deflecting of inherited tendencies.

Her fears were in a measure confirmed by the first two years of their life in New York, and the opening of his career as a professional architect. Close on the easy triumphs of his studentships there came the chilling reaction of public indifference. Dick, on his return from Paris, had formed a partnership with an architect who had had several years of practical training in a New York office; but the quiet and industrious Gill, though he attracted to the new firm a few small jobs which overflowed from the business of his former employer, was not able to infect the public with his own faith in Peyton's talents, and it was trying to a genius who felt himself capable of creating palaces to have to restrict his efforts to the building of suburban cottages or the planning of cheap alterations in private houses.

Mrs. Peyton expended all the ingenuities of tenderness in keeping up her son's courage; and she was seconded in the task by a friend whose acquaintance Dick had made at the Beaux Arts, and who, two years before the Peytons, had returned to New York to start on his own career as an architect. Paul Darrow was a young man full of crude seriousness, who, after a youth of struggling work and study in his native northwestern state, had won a scholarship which sent him abroad for a course at the Beaux Arts. His two years there coincided with the first part of Dick's residence, and Darrow's gifts had at once attracted the younger student. Dick was unstinted in his admiration of rival talent, and Mrs. Peyton, who was romantically given to the cultivation of such generosities, had seconded his enthusiasm by the kindest offers of hospitality to the young student. Darrow thus became the grateful frequenter of their little salon; and after their return to New York the intimacy between the young men was renewed, though Mrs. Peyton found it more difficult to coax Dick's friend to her New York drawing-room than to the informal surroundings of the Rue de Varennes. There, no doubt, secluded and absorbed in her son's work, she had seemed to Darrow almost a fellow-student; but seen among her own associates she became once more the woman of fashion, divided from him by the whole breadth of her ease and his awkwardness. Mrs. Peyton, whose tact had divined the cause of his estrangement, would not for an instant let it affect the friendship of the two young men. She encouraged Dick to frequent Darrow, in whom she divined a persistency of effort, an artistic self-confidence, in curious contrast to his social hesitancies. The example of his obstinate capacity for work was just the influence her son needed, and if Darrow would not come to them she insisted that Dick must seek him out, must never let him think that any social discrepancy could affect a friendship based on deeper things. Dick, who had all the loyalties, and who took an honest pride in his friend's growing success, needed no urging to maintain the intimacy; and his copious reports of midnight colloquies in Darrow's lodgings showed Mrs. Peyton that she had a strong ally in her invisible friend.

It had been, therefore, somewhat of a shock to learn in the course of time that Darrow's influence was being shared, if not counteracted, by that of a young lady in whose honour Dick was now giving his first professional tea. Mrs. Peyton had heard a great deal about Miss Clemence Verney, first from the usual purveyors of such information, and more recently from her son, who, probably divining that rumour had been before him, adopted his usual method of disarming his mother by taking her into his confidence. But, ample as her information was, it remained perplexing and contradictory, and even her own few meetings with the girl had not helped her to a definite opinion. Miss Verney, in conduct and ideas, was patently of the "new school": a young woman of feverish activities and broad-cast judgments, whose very versatility made her hard to define. Mrs. Peyton was shrewd enough to allow for the accidents of environment; what she wished to get at was the residuum of character beneath Miss Verney's shifting surface.

"It looks charmingly," Mrs. Peyton repeated, giving a loosening touch to the chrysanthemums in a tall vase on her son's desk.

Dick laughed, and glanced at his watch.

"They won't be here for another quarter of an hour. I think I'll tell Gill to clean out the work-room before they come."

"Are we to see the drawings for the competition?" his mother asked.

He shook his head smilingly. "Can't—I've asked one or two of the Beaux Arts fellows, you know; and besides, old Darrow's actually coming."

"Impossible!" Mrs. Peyton exclaimed.

"He swore he would last night." Dick laughed again, with a tinge of self-satisfaction. "I've an idea he wants to see Miss Verney."

"Ah," his mother murmured. There was a pause before she added: "Has Darrow really gone in for this competition?"

"Rather! I should say so! He's simply working himself to the bone."

Mrs. Peyton sat revolving her muff on a meditative hand; at length she said: "I'm not sure I think it quite nice of him."

Her son halted before her with an incredulous stare. "Mother!" he exclaimed.

The rebuke sent a blush to her forehead. "Well, considering your friendship, and everything."

"Everything? What do you mean by everything? The fact that he had more ability than I have and is therefore more likely to succeed? The fact that he needs the money and the success a deuced sight more than any of us? Is that the reason you think he oughtn't to have entered? Mother! I never heard you say an ungenerous thing before."

The blush deepened to crimson, and she rose with a nervous laugh. "It was ungenerous," she conceded. "I suppose I'm jealous for you. I hate these competitions!"

Her son smiled reassuringly. "You needn't. I'm not afraid: I think I shall pull it off this time. In fact, Paul's the only man I'm afraid of, I'm always afraid of Paul, but the mere fact that he's in the thing is a tremendous stimulus."

His mother continued to study him with an anxious tenderness. "Have you worked out the whole scheme? Do you see it yet?"

"Oh, broadly, yes. There's a gap here and there, a hazy bit, rather, it's the hardest problem I've ever had to tackle; but then it's my biggest opportunity, and I've simply got to pull it off!"

Mrs. Peyton sat silent, considering his flushed face and illumined eye, which were rather those of the victor nearing the goal than of the runner just beginning the race. She remembered something that Darrow had once said of him: "Dick always sees the end too soon."

"You haven't too much time left," she murmured.

"Just a week. But I shan't go anywhere after this. I shall renounce the world." He glanced smilingly at the festal tea-table and the embowered desk. "When I next appear, it will either be with my heel on Paul's neck, poor old Paul—or else—or else—being dragged lifeless from the arena!"

His mother nervously took up the laugh with which he ended. "Oh, not lifeless," she said.

His face clouded. "Well, maimed for life, then," he muttered.

Mrs. Peyton made no answer. She knew how much hung on the possibility of his whining the competition which for weeks past had engrossed him. It was a design for the new museum of sculpture, for which the city had recently voted half a million. Dick's taste ran naturally to the grandiose, and the erection of public buildings had always been the object of his ambition. Here was an unmatched opportunity, and he knew that, in a competition of the kind, the newest man had as much chance of success as the firm of most established reputation, since every competitor entered on his own merits, the designs being submitted to a jury of architects who voted on them without knowing the names of the contestants. Dick, characteristically, was not afraid of the older firms; indeed, as he had told his mother, Paul Darrow was the only rival he feared. Mrs. Peyton knew that, to a certain point, self-confidence was a good sign; but somehow her son's did not strike her as being of the right substance, it seemed to have no dimension but extent. Her fears were complicated by a suspicion that, under his professional eagerness for success, lay the knowledge that Miss Verney's favour hung on the victory. It was that, perhaps, which gave a feverish touch to his ambition; and Mrs. Peyton, surveying the future from the height of her material apprehensions, divined that the situation depended mainly on the girl's view of it. She would have given a great deal to know Clemence Verney's conception of success.

Miss Verney, when she presently appeared, in the wake of the impersonal and exclamatory young married woman who served as a background to her vivid outline, seemed competent to impart at short notice any information required of her. She had never struck Mrs. Peyton as more alert and efficient. A melting grace of line and colour tempered her edges with the charming haze of youth; but it occurred to her critic that she might emerge from this morning mist as a dry and metallic old woman.

If Miss Verney suspected a personal application in Dick's hospitality, it did not call forth in her the usual tokens of self-consciousness. Her manner may have been a shade more vivid than usual, but she preserved all her bright composure of glance and speech, so that one guessed, under the rapid dispersal of words, an undisturbed steadiness of perception. She was lavishly but not indiscriminately interested in the evidences of her host's industry, and as the other guests assembled, straying with vague ejaculations through the labyrinth of scale drawings and blue prints, Mrs. Peyton noted that Miss Verney alone knew what these symbols stood for.

To his visitors' requests to be shown his plans for the competition, Peyton had opposed a laughing refusal, enforced by the presence of two fellow-architects, young men with lingering traces of the Beaux Arts in their costume and vocabulary, who stood about in Gavarni attitudes and dazzled the ladies by allusions to fenestration and entasis. The party had already drifted back to the tea-table when a hesitating knock announced Darrow's approach. He entered with his usual air of having blundered in by mistake, embarrassed by his hat and great-coat, and thrown into deeper confusion by the necessity of being introduced to the ladies grouped about the urn. To the men he threw a gruff nod of fellowship, and Dick having relieved him of his encumbrances, he retreated behind the shelter of Mrs. Peyton's welcome. The latter judiciously gave him time to recover, and when she turned to him he was engaged in a surreptitious inspection of Miss Verney, whose dusky slenderness, relieved against the bare walls of the office, made her look like a young St. John of Donatello's. The girl returned his look with one of her clear glances, and the group having presently broken up again, Mrs. Peyton saw that she had drifted to Darrow's side. The visitors at length wandered back to the work-room to see a portfolio of Dick's water-colours; but Mrs. Peyton remained seated behind the urn, listening to the interchange of talk through the open door while she tried to coordinate her impressions.

She saw that Miss Verney was sincerely interested in Dick's work: it was the nature of her interest that remained in doubt. As if to solve this doubt, the girl presently reappeared alone on the threshold, and discovering Mrs. Peyton, advanced toward her with a smile.

"Are you tired of hearing us praise Mr. Peyton's things?" she asked, dropping into a low chair beside her hostess. "Unintelligent admiration must be a bore to people who know, and Mr. Darrow tells me you are almost as learned as your son."

Mrs. Peyton returned the smile, but evaded the question. "I should be sorry to think your admiration unintelligent," she said. "I like to feel that my boy's work is appreciated by people who understand it."

"Oh, I have the usual smattering," said Miss Verney carelessly. "I think I know why I admire his work; but then I am sure I see more in it when some one like Mr. Darrow tells me how remarkable it is."

"Does Mr. Darrow say that?" the mother exclaimed, losing sight of her object in the rush of maternal pleasure.

"He has said nothing else: it seems to be the only subject which loosens his tongue. I believe he is more anxious to have your son win the competition than to win it himself."

"He is a very good friend," Mrs. Peyton assented. She was struck by the way in which the girl led the topic back to the special application of it which interested her. She had none of the artifices of prudery.

"He feels sure that Mr. Peyton will win," Miss Verney continued. "It was very interesting to hear his reasons. He is an extraordinarily interesting man. It must be a tremendous incentive to have such a friend."

Mrs. Peyton hesitated. "The friendship is delightful; but I don't know that my son needs the incentive. He is almost too ambitious."

Miss Verney looked up brightly. "Can one be?" she said. "Ambition is so splendid! It must be so glorious to be a man and go crashing through obstacles, straight up to the thing one is after. I'm afraid I don't care for people who are superior to success. I like marriage by capture!" She rose with her wandering laugh, and stood flushed and sparkling above Mrs. Peyton, who continued to gaze at her gravely.

"What do you call success?" the latter asked. "It means so many different things."

"Oh, yes, I know, the inward approval, and all that. Well, I'm afraid I like the other kind: the drums and wreaths and acclamations. If I were Mr. Peyton, for instance, I'd much rather win the competition than—than be as disinterested as Mr. Darrow."

Mrs. Peyton smiled. "I hope you won't tell him so," she said half seriously. "He is over-stimulated already; and he is so easily influenced by any one who—whose opinion he values."

She stopped abruptly, hearing herself, with a strange inward shock, re-echo the words which another man's mother had once spoken to her. Miss Verney did not seem to take the allusion to herself, for she continued to fix on Mrs. Peyton a gaze of impartial sympathy.

"But we can't help being interested!" she declared.

"It's very kind of you; but I wish you would all help him to feel that his competition is after all of very little account compared with other things, his health and his peace of mind, for instance. He is looking horribly used up."

The girl glanced over her shoulder at Dick, who was just reentering the room at Darrow's side.

"Oh, do you think so?" she said. "I should have thought it was his friend who was used up."

Mrs. Peyton followed the glance with surprise. She had been too preoccupied to notice Darrow, whose crudely modelled face was always of a dull pallour, to which his slow-moving grey eye lent no relief except in rare moments of expansion. Now the face had the fallen lines of a death-mask, in which only the smile he turned on Dick remained alive; and the sight smote her with compunction. Poor Darrow! He did look horribly fagged out: as if he needed care and petting and good food. No one knew exactly how he lived. His rooms, according to Dick's report, were fireless and ill kept, but he stuck to them because his landlady, whom he had fished out of some financial plight, had difficulty in obtaining other lodgers. He belonged to no clubs, and wandered out alone for his meals, mysteriously refusing the hospitality which his friends pressed on him. It was plain that he was very poor, and Dick conjectured that he sent what he earned to an aunt in his native village; but he was so silent about such matters that, outside of his profession, he seemed to have no personal life.

Miss Verney's companion having presently advised her of the lapse of time, there ensued a general leave-taking, at the close of which Dick accompanied the ladies to their carriage. Darrow was meanwhile blundering into his greatcoat, a process which always threw him into a state of perspiring embarrassment; but Mrs. Peyton, surprising him in the act, suggested that he should defer it and give her a few moments' talk.

"Let me make you some fresh tea," she said, as Darrow blushingly shed the garment, "and when Dick comes back we'll all walk home together. I've not had a chance to say two words to you this winter."

Darrow sank into a chair at her side and nervously contemplated his boots. "I've been tremendously hard at work," he said.

"I know: too hard at work, I'm afraid. Dick tells me you have been wearing yourself out over your competition plans."

"Oh, well, I shall have time to rest now," he returned. "I put the last stroke to them this morning."

Mrs. Peyton gave him a quick look. "You're ahead of Dick, then."

"In point of time only," he said smiling.

"That is in itself an advantage," she answered with a tinge of asperity. In spite of an honest effort for impartiality she could not, at the moment, help regarding Darrow as an obstacle in her son's path.

"I wish the competition were over!" she exclaimed, conscious that her voice had betrayed her. "I hate to see you both looking so fagged."

Darrow smiled again, perhaps at her studied inclusion of himself.

"Oh, Dick's all right," he said. "He'll pull himself together in no time."

He spoke with an emphasis which might have struck her, if her sympathies had not again been deflected by the allusion to her son.

"Not if he doesn't win," she exclaimed.

Darrow took the tea she had poured for him, knocking the spoon to the floor in his eagerness to perform the feat gracefully. In bending to recover the spoon he struck the tea-table with his shoulder, and set the cups dancing. Having regained a measure of composure, he took a swallow of the hot tea and set it down with a gasp, precariously near the edge of the tea-table. Mrs. Peyton rescued the cup, and Darrow, apparently forgetting its existence, rose and began to pace the room. It was always hard for him to sit still when he talked.

"You mean he's so tremendously set on it?" he broke out.

Mrs. Peyton hesitated. "You know him almost as well as I do," she said. "He's capable of anything where there is a possibility of success; but I'm always afraid of the reaction."

"Oh, well, Dick's a man," said Darrow bluntly. "Besides, he's going to succeed."

"I wish he didn't feel so sure of it. You mustn't think I'm afraid for him. He's a man, and I want him to take his chances with other men; but I wish he didn't care so much about what people think."

"People?"

"Miss Verney, then: I suppose you know."

Darrow paused in front of her. "Yes: he's talked a good deal about her. You think she wants him to succeed?"

"At any price!"

He drew his brows together. "What do you call any price?"

"Well, herself, in this case, I believe."

Darrow bent a puzzled stare on her. "You mean she attached that amount of importance to this competition?"

"She seems to regard it as symbolical: that's what I gather. And I'm afraid she's given him the same impression."

Darrow's sunken face was suffused by his rare smile. "Oh, well, he'll pull it off then!" he said.

Mrs. Peyton rose with a distracted sigh. "I half hope he won't, for such a motive," she exclaimed.

"The motive won't show in his work," said Darrow. He added, after a pause probably devoted to the search for the right word: "He seems to think a great deal of her."

Mrs. Peyton fixed him thoughtfully. "I wish I knew what you think of her."

"Why, I never saw her before."

"No; but you talked with her to-day. You've formed an opinion: I think you came here on purpose."

He chuckled joyously at her discernment: she had always seemed to him gifted with supernatural insight. "Well, I did want to see her," he owned.

"And what do you think?"

He took a few vague steps and then halted before Mrs. Peyton. "I think," he said, smiling, "that she likes to be helped first, and to have everything on her plate at once."

III

At dinner, with a rush of contrition, Mrs. Peyton remembered that she had after all not spoken to Darrow about his health. He had distracted her by beginning to talk of Dick; and besides, much as Darrow's opinions interested her, his personality had never fixed her attention. He always seemed to her simply a vehicle for the transmission of ideas.

It was Dick who recalled her to a sense of her omission by asking if she hadn't thought that old Paul looked rather more ragged than usual.

"He did look tired," Mrs. Peyton conceded. "I meant to tell him to take care of himself."

Dick laughed at the futility of the measure. "Old Paul is never tired: he can work twenty-five hours out of the twenty-four. The trouble with him is that he's ill. Something wrong with the machinery, I'm afraid."

"Oh, I'm sorry. Has he seen a doctor?"

"He wouldn't listen to me when I suggested it the other day; but he's so deuced mysterious that I don't know what he may have done since." Dick rose, putting down his coffee-cup and half-smoked cigarette. "I've half a mind to pop in on him tonight and see how he's getting on."

"But he lives at the other end of the earth; and you're tired yourself."

"I'm not tired; only a little strung-up," he returned, smiling. "And besides, I'm going to meet Gill at the office by and by and put in a night's work. It won't hurt me to take a look at Paul first."

Mrs. Peyton was silent. She knew it was useless to contend with her son about his work, and she tried to fortify herself with the remembrance of her own words to Darrow: Dick was a man and must take his chance with other men.

But Dick, glancing at his watch, uttered an exclamation of annoyance. "Oh, by Jove, I shan't have time after all. Gill is waiting for me now; we must have dawdled over dinner." He went to give his mother a caressing tap on the cheek. "Now don't worry," he adjured her; and as she smiled back at him he added with a sudden happy blush: "She doesn't, you know: she's so sure of me."

Mrs. Peyton's smile faded, and laying a detaining hand on his, she said with sudden directness: "Sure of you, or of your success?"

He hesitated. "Oh, she regards them as synonymous. She thinks I'm bound to get on."

"But if you don't?"

He shrugged laughingly, but with a slight contraction of his confident brows. "Why, I shall have to make way for some one else, I suppose. That's the law of life."

Mrs. Peyton sat upright, gazing at him with a kind of solemnity. "Is it the law of love?" she asked.

He looked down on her with a smile that trembled a little. "My dear romantic mother, I don't want her pity, you know!"

Dick, coming home the next morning shortly before daylight, left the house again after a hurried breakfast, and Mrs. Peyton heard nothing of him till nightfall. He had promised to be back for dinner, but a few moments before eight, as she was coming down to the drawing-room, the parlour-maid handed her a hastily pencilled note.

"Don't wait for me," it ran. "Darrow is ill and I can't leave him. I'll send a line when the doctor has seen him."

Mrs. Peyton, who was a woman of rapid reactions, read the words with a pang. She was ashamed of the jealous thoughts she had harboured of Darrow, and of the selfishness which had made her lose sight of his troubles in the consideration of Dick's welfare. Even Clemence Verney, whom she secretly accused of a want of heart, had been struck by Darrow's ill looks, while she had had eyes only for her son. Poor Darrow! How cold and self-engrossed he must have thought her! In the first rush of penitence her impulse was to drive at once to his lodgings; but the infection of his own shyness restrained her. Dick's note gave no details; the illness was evidently grave, but might not Darrow regard her coming as an intrusion? To repair her negligence of yesterday by a sudden invasion of his privacy might be only a greater failure in tact; and after a moment of deliberation she resolved on sending to ask Dick if he wished her to go to him.

The reply, which came late, was what she had expected. "No, we have all the help we need. The doctor has sent a good nurse, and is coming again later. It's pneumonia, but of course he doesn't say much yet. Let me have some beef-juice as soon as the cook can make it."

The beef-juice ordered and dispatched, she was left to a vigil in melancholy contrast to that of the previous evening. Then she had been enclosed in the narrow limits of her maternal interests; now the barriers of self were broken down, and her personal preoccupations swept away on the current of a wider sympathy. As she sat there in the radius of lamp-light which, for so many evenings, had held Dick and herself in a charmed circle of tenderness, she saw that her love for her boy had come to be merely a kind of extended egotism. Love had narrowed instead of widening her, had rebuilt between herself and life the very walls which, years and years before, she had laid low with bleeding fingers. It was horrible, how she had come to sacrifice everything to the one passion of ambition for her boy....

At daylight she sent another messenger, one of her own servants, who returned without having seen Dick. Mr. Peyton had sent word that there was no change. He would write later; he wanted nothing. The day wore on drearily. Once Kate found herself computing the precious hours lost to Dick's unfinished task. She blushed at her ineradicable selfishness, and tried to turn her mind to poor Darrow. But she could not master her impulses; and now she caught herself indulging the thought that his illness would at least exclude him from the competition. But no, she remembered that he had said his work was finished. Come what might, he stood in the path of her boy's success. She hated herself for the thought, but it would not down.

Evening drew on, but there was no note from Dick. At length, in the shamed reaction from her fears, she rang for a carriage and went upstairs to dress. She could stand aloof no longer: she must go to Darrow, if only to escape from her wicked thoughts of him. As she came down again she heard Dick's key in the door. She hastened her steps, and as she reached the hall he stood before her without speaking.

She looked at him and the question died on her lips. He nodded, and walked slowly past her.

"There was no hope from the first," he said.

The next day Dick was taken up with the preparations for the funeral. The distant aunt, who appeared to be Darrow's only relation, had been duly notified of his death; but no answer having been received from her, it was left to his friend to fulfil the customary duties. He was again absent for the best part of the day; and when he returned at dusk Mrs. Peyton, looking up from the tea-table behind which she awaited him, was startled by the deep-lined misery of his face.

Her own thoughts were too painful for ready expression, and they sat for a while in a mute community of wretchedness.

"Is everything arranged?" she asked at length.

"Yes. Everything."

"And you have not heard from the aunt?"

He shook his head.

"Can you find no trace of any other relations?"

"None. I went over all his papers. There were very few, and I found no address but the aunt's." He sat thrown back in his chair, disregarding the cup of tea she had mechanically poured for him. "I found this, though," he added, after a pause, drawing a letter from his pocket and holding it out to her.

She took it doubtfully. "Ought I to read it?"

"Yes."

She saw then that the envelope, in Darrow's hand, was addressed to her son. Within were a few pencilled words, dated on the first day of his illness, the morrow of the day on which she had last seen him.

"Dear Dick," she read, "I want you to use my plans for the museum if you can get any good out of them. Even if I pull out of this I want you to. I shall have other chances, and I have an idea this one means a lot to you."

Mrs. Peyton sat speechless, gazing at the date of the letter, which she had instantly connected with her last talk with Darrow. She saw that he had understood her, and the thought scorched her to the soul.

"Wasn't it glorious of him?" Dick said.

She dropped the letter, and hid her face in her hands.

IV

The funeral took place the next morning, and on the return from the cemetery Dick told his mother that he must go and look over things at Darrow's office. He had heard the day before from his friend's aunt, a helpless person to whom telegraphy was difficult and travel inconceivable, and who, in eight pages of unpunctuated eloquence, made over to Dick what she called the melancholy privilege of winding up her nephew's affairs.

Mrs. Peyton looked anxiously at her son. "Is there no one who can do this for you? He must have had a clerk or some one who knows about his work."

Dick shook his head. "Not lately. He hasn't had much to do this winter, and these last months he had chucked everything to work alone over his plans."

The word brought a faint colour to Mrs. Peyton's cheek. It was the first allusion that either of them had made to Darrow's bequest.

"Oh, of course you must do all you can," she murmured, turning alone into the house.

The emotions of the morning had stirred her deeply, and she sat at home during the day, letting her mind dwell, in a kind of retrospective piety, on the thought of poor Darrow's devotion. She had given him too little time while he lived, had acquiesced too easily in his growing habits of seclusion; and she felt it as a proof of insensibility that she had not been more closely drawn to the one person who had loved Dick as she loved him. The evidence of that love, as shown in Darrow's letter, filled her with a vain compunction. The very extravagance of his offer lent it a deeper pathos. It was wonderful that, even in the urgency of affection, a man of his almost morbid rectitude should have overlooked the restrictions of professional honour, should have implied the possibility of his friend's overlooking them. It seemed to make his sacrifice the more complete that it had, unconsciously, taken the form of a subtle temptation.

The last word arrested Mrs. Peyton's thoughts. A temptation? To whom? Not, surely, to one capable, as her son was capable, of rising to the height of his friend's devotion. The offer, to Dick, would mean simply, as it meant to her, the last touching expression of an inarticulate fidelity: the utterance of a love which at last had found its formula. Mrs. Peyton dismissed as morbid any other view of the case. She was annoyed with herself for supposing that Dick could be ever so remotely affected by the possibility at which poor Darrow's renunciation hinted. The nature of the offer removed it from practical issues to the idealizing region of sentiment.

Mrs. Peyton had been sitting alone with these thoughts for the greater part of the afternoon, and dusk was falling when Dick entered the drawing-room. In the dim light, with his pallour heightened by the sombre effect of his mourning, he came upon her almost startlingly, with a revival of some long-effaced impression which, for a moment, gave her the sense of struggling among shadows. She did not, at first, know what had produced the effect; then she saw that it was his likeness to his father.

"Well, is it over?" she asked, as he threw himself into a chair without speaking.

"Yes: I've looked through everything." He leaned back, crossing his hands behind his head, and gazing past her with a look of utter lassitude.

She paused a moment, and then said tentatively: "Tomorrow you will be able to go back to your work."

"Oh, my work," he exclaimed, as if to brush aside an ill-timed pleasantry.

"Are you too tired?"

"No." He rose and began to wander up and down the room. "I'm not tired. Give me some tea, will you?" He paused before her while she poured the cup, and then, without taking it, turned away to light a cigarette.

"Surely there is still time?" she suggested, with her eyes on him.

"Time? To finish my plans? Oh, yes, there's time. But they're not worth it."

"Not worth it?" She started up, and then dropped back into her seat, ashamed of having betrayed her anxiety. "They are worth as much as they were last week," she said with an attempt at cheerfulness.

"Not to me," he returned. "I hadn't seen Darrow's then."

There was a long silence. Mrs. Peyton sat with her eyes fixed on her clasped hands, and her son paced the room restlessly.

"Are they so wonderful?" she asked at length.

"Yes."

She paused again, and then said, lifting a tremulous glance to his face: "That makes his offer all the more beautiful."

Dick was lighting another cigarette, and his face was turned from her. "Yes, I suppose so," he said in a low tone.

"They were quite finished, he told me," she continued, unconsciously dropping her voice to the pitch of his.

"Yes."

"Then they will be entered, I suppose?"

"Of course, why not?" he answered almost sharply.

"Shall you have time to attend to all that and to finish yours too?"

"Oh, I suppose so. I've told you it isn't a question of tune. I see now that mine are not worth bothering with."

She rose and approached him, laying her hands on his shoulders. "You are tired and unstrung; how can you judge? Why not let me look at both designs to-morrow?"

Under her gaze he flushed abruptly and drew back with a half-impatient gesture.

"Oh, I'm afraid that wouldn't help me; you'd be sure to think mine best," he said with a laugh.

"But if I could give you good reasons?" she pressed him.

He took her hand, as if ashamed of his impatience. "Dear mother, if you had any reasons their mere existence would prove that they were bad."

His mother did not return his smile. "You won't let me see the two designs then?" she said with a faint tinge of insistence.

"Oh, of course, if you want to, if you only won't talk about it now! Can't you see that I'm pretty nearly dead-beat?" he burst out uncontrollably; and as she stood silent, he added with a weary fall in his voice, "I think I'll go upstairs and see if I can't get a nap before dinner."

Though they had separated upon the assurance that she should see the two designs if she wished it, Mrs. Peyton knew they would not be shown to her. Dick, indeed, would not again deny her request; but had he not reckoned on the improbability of her renewing it? All night she lay confronted by that question. The situation shaped itself before her with that hallucinating distinctness which belongs to the midnight vision. She knew now why Dick had suddenly reminded her of his father: had she not once before seen the same thought moving behind the same eyes? She was sure it had occurred to Dick to use Darrow's drawings. As she lay awake in the darkness she could hear him, long after midnight, pacing the floor overhead: she held her breath, listening to the recurring beat of his foot, which seemed that of an imprisoned spirit revolving wearily in the cage of the same thought. She felt in every fibre that a crisis in her son's life had been reached, that the act now before him would have a determining effect on his whole future. The circumstances of her past had raised to clairvoyance her natural insight into human motive, had made of her a moral barometer responding to the faintest fluctuations of atmosphere, and years of anxious meditation had familiarized her with the form which her son's temptations were likely to take. The peculiar misery of her situation was that she could not, except indirectly, put this intuition, this foresight, at his service. It was a part of her discernment to be aware that life is the only real counsellor, that wisdom unfiltered through personal experience does not become a part of the moral tissues. Love such as hers had a great office, the office of preparation and direction; but it must know how to hold its hand and keep its counsel, how to attend upon its object as an invisible influence rather than as an active interference.

All this Kate Peyton had told herself again and again, during those hours of anxious calculation in which she had tried to cast Dick's horoscope; but not in her moments of most fantastic foreboding had she figured so cruel a test of her courage. If her prayers for him had taken precise shape, she might have asked that he should be spared the spectacular, the dramatic appeal to his will-power: that his temptations should slip by him in a dull disguise. She had secured him against all ordinary forms of baseness; the vulnerable point lay higher, in that region of idealizing egotism which is the seat of life in such natures.

Years of solitary foresight gave her mind a singular alertness in dealing with such possibilities. She saw at once that the peril of the situation lay in the minimum of risk it involved. Darrow had employed no assistant in working out his plans for the competition, and his secluded life made it almost certain that he had not shown them to any one, and that she and Dick alone knew them to have been completed. Moreover, it was a part of Dick's duty to examine the contents of his friend's office, and in doing this nothing would be easier than to possess himself of the drawings and make use of any part of them that might serve his purpose. He had Darrow's authority for doing so; and though the act involved a slight breach of professional probity, might not his friend's wishes be invoked as a secret justification? Mrs. Peyton found herself almost hating poor Darrow for having been the unconscious instrument of her son's temptation. But what right had she, after all, to suspect Dick of considering, even for a moment, the act of which she was so ready to accuse him? His unwillingness to let her see the drawings might have been the accidental result of lassitude and discouragement. He was tired and troubled, and she had chosen the wrong moment to make the request. His want of readiness might even be due to the wish to conceal from her how far his friend had surpassed him. She knew his sensitiveness on this point, and reproached herself for not having foreseen it. But her own arguments failed to convince her. Deep beneath her love for her boy and her faith in him there lurked a nameless doubt. She could hardly now, in looking back, define the impulse upon which she had married Denis Peyton: she knew only that the deeps of her nature had been loosened, and that she had been borne forward on their current to the very fate from which her heart recoiled. But if in one sense her marriage remained a problem, there was another in which her motherhood seemed to solve it. She had never lost the sense of having snatched her child from some dim peril which still lurked and hovered; and he became more closely hers with every effort of her vigilant love. For the act of rescue had not been accomplished once and for all in the moment of immolation: it had not been by a sudden stroke of heroism, but by ever-renewed and indefatigable effort, that she had built up for him the miraculous shelter of her love. And now that it stood there, a hallowed refuge against failure, she could not even set a light in the pane, but must let him grope his way to it unaided.

V

Mrs. Peyton's midnight musings summed themselves up in the conclusion that the next few hours would end her uncertainty. She felt the day to be decisive. If Dick offered to show her the drawings, her fears would be proved groundless; if he avoided the subject, they were justified.

She dressed early in order not to miss him at breakfast; but as she entered the dining-room the parlour-maid told her that Mr. Peyton had overslept himself, and had rung to have his breakfast sent upstairs. Was it a pretext to avoid her? She was vexed at her own readiness to see a portent in the simplest incident; but while she blushed at her doubts she let them govern her. She left the dining-room door open, determined not to miss him if he came downstairs while she was at breakfast; then she went back to the drawing-room and sat down at her writing-table, trying to busy herself with some accounts while she listened for his step. Here too she had left the door open; but presently even this slight departure from her daily usage seemed a deviation from the passive attitude she had adopted, and she rose and shut the door. She knew that she could still hear his step on the stairs, he had his father's quick swinging gait, but as she sat listening, and vainly trying to write, the closed door seemed to symbolize a refusal to share in his trial, a hardening of herself against his need of her. What if he should come down intending to speak, and should be turned from his purpose? Slighter obstacles have deflected the course of events in those indeterminate moments when the soul floats between two tides. She sprang up quickly, and as her hand touched the latch she heard his step on the stairs.

When he entered the drawing-room she had regained the writing-table and could lift a composed face to his. He came in hurriedly, yet with a kind of reluctance beneath his haste: again it was his father's step. She smiled, but looked away from him as he approached her; she seemed to be re-living her own past as one re-lives things in the distortion of fever.

"Are you off already?" she asked, glancing at the hat in his hand.

"Yes; I'm late as it is. I overslept myself." He paused and looked vaguely about the room. "Don't expect me till late, don't wait dinner for me."

She stirred impulsively. "Dick, you're overworking, you'll make yourself ill."

"Nonsense. I'm as fit as ever this morning. Don't be imagining things."

He dropped his habitual kiss on her forehead, and turned to go. On the threshold he paused, and she felt that something in him sought her and then drew back. "Good-bye," he called to her as the door closed on him.

She sat down and tried to survey the situation divested of her midnight fears. He had not referred to her wish to see the drawings: but what did the omission signify? Might he not have forgotten her request? Was she not forcing the most trivial details to fit in with her apprehensions? Unfortunately for her own reassurance, she knew that her familiarity with Dick's processes was based on such minute observation, and that, to such intimacy as theirs, no indications were trivial. She was as certain as if he had spoken, that when he had left the house that morning he was weighing the possibility of using Darrow's drawings, of supplementing his own incomplete design from the fulness of his friend's invention. And with a bitter pang she divined that he was sorry he had shown her Darrow's letter.

It was impossible to remain face to face with such conjectures, and though she had given up all her engagements during the few days since Darrow's death, she now took refuge in the thought of a concert which was to take place at a friend's house that morning. The music-room, when she entered, was thronged with acquaintances, and she found transient relief in that dispersal of attention which makes society an anesthetic for some forms of wretchedness. Contact with the pressure of busy indifferent life often gives remoteness to questions which have clung as close as the flesh to the bone; and if Mrs. Peyton did not find such complete release, she at least interposed between herself and her anxiety the obligation to dissemble it. But the relief was only momentary, and when the first bars of the overture turned from her the smiles of recognition among which she had tried to lose herself, she felt a deeper sense of isolation. The music, which at another time would have swept her away on some rich current of emotion, now seemed to island her in her own thoughts, to create an artificial solitude in which she found herself more immitigably face to face with her fears. The silence, the recueillement, about her gave resonance to the inner voices, lucidity to the inner vision, till she seemed enclosed in a luminous empty horizon against which every possibility took the sharp edge of accomplished fact. With relentless precision the course of events was unrolled before her: she saw Dick yielding to his opportunity, snatching victory from dishonour, winning love, happiness and success in the act by which he lost himself. It was all so simple, so easy, so inevitable, that she felt the futility of struggling or hoping against it. He would win the competition, would marry Miss Verney, would press on to achievement through the opening which the first success had made for him.

As Mrs. Peyton reached this point in her forecast, she found her outward gaze arrested by the face of the young lady who so dominated her inner vision. Miss Verney, a few rows distant, sat intent upon the music, in that attitude of poised motion which was her nearest approach to repose. Her slender brown profile with its breezy hair, her quick eye, and the lips which seemed to listen as well as speak, all betokened to Mrs. Peyton a nature through which the obvious energies blew free, a bare open stretch of consciousness without shelter for tenderer growths. She shivered to think of Dick's frail scruples exposed to those rustling airs. And then, suddenly, a new thought struck her. What if she might turn this force to her own use, make it serve, unconsciously to Dick, as the means of his deliverance? Hitherto she had assumed that her son's worst danger lay in the chance of his confiding his difficulty to Clemence Verney; and she had, in her own past, a precedent which made her think such a confidence not unlikely. If he did carry his scruples to the girl, she argued, the latter's imperviousness, her frank inability to understand them, would have the effect of dispelling them like mist; and he was acute enough to know this and profit by it. So she had hitherto reasoned; but now the girl's presence seemed to clarify her perceptions, and she told herself that something in Dick's nature, something which she herself had put there, would resist this short cut to safety, would make him take the more tortuous way to his goal rather than gain it through the privacies of the heart he loved. For she had lifted him thus far above his father, that it would be a disenchantment to him to find that Clemence Verney did not share his scruples. On this much, his mother now exultingly felt, she could count in her passive struggle for supremacy. No, he would never, never tell Clemence Verney, and his one hope, his sure salvation, therefore lay in some one else's telling her.

The excitement of this discovery had nearly, in mid-concert, swept Mrs. Peyton from her seat to the girl's side. Fearing to miss the latter in the throng at the entrance, she slipped out during the last number and, lingering in the farther drawing-room, let the dispersing audience drift her in Miss Verney's direction. The girl shone sympathetically on her approach, and in a moment they had detached themselves from the crowd and taken refuge in the perfumed emptiness of the conservatory.

The girl, whose sensations were always easily set in motion, had at first a good deal to say of the music, for which she claimed, on her hearer's part, an active show of approval or dissent; but this dismissed, she turned a melting face on Mrs. Peyton and said with one of her rapid modulations of tone: "I was so sorry about poor Mr. Darrow."

Mrs. Peyton uttered an assenting sigh. "It was a great grief to us, a great loss to my son."

"Yes, I know. I can imagine what you must have felt. And then it was so unlucky that it should have happened just now."

Mrs. Peyton shot a reconnoitring glance at her profile. "His dying, you mean, on the eve of success?"

Miss Verney turned a frank smile upon her. "One ought to feel that, of course, but I'm afraid I am very selfish where my friends are concerned, and I was thinking of Mr. Peyton's having to give up his work at such a critical moment." She spoke without a note of deprecation: there was a pagan freshness in her opportunism.

Mrs. Peyton was silent, and the girl continued after a pause: "I suppose now it will be almost impossible for him to finish his drawings in time. It's a pity he hadn't worked out the whole scheme a little sooner. Then the details would have come of themselves."

Mrs. Peyton felt a contempt strangely mingled with exultation. If only the girl would talk in that way to Dick!

"He has hardly had time to think of himself lately," she said, trying to keep the coldness out of her voice.

"No, of course not," Miss Verney assented; "but isn't that all the more reason for his friends to think of him? It was very dear of him to give up everything to nurse Mr. Darrow, but, after all, if a man is going to get on in his career there are times when he must think first of himself."

Mrs. Peyton paused, trying to choose her words with deliberation. It was quite clear now that Dick had not spoken, and she felt the responsibility that devolved upon her.

"Getting on in a career, is that always the first thing to be considered?" she asked, letting her eyes rest musingly on the girl's.

The glance did not disconcert Miss Verney, who returned it with one of equal comprehensiveness. "Yes," she said quickly, and with a slight blush. "With a temperament like Mr. Peyton's I believe it is. Some people can pick themselves up after any number of bad falls: I am not sure that he could. I think discouragement would weaken instead of strengthening him."

Both women had forgotten external conditions in the quick reach for each other's meanings. Mrs. Peyton flushed, her maternal pride in revolt; but the answer was checked on her lips by the sense of the girl's unexpected insight. Here was some one who knew Dick as well as she did, should she say a partisan or an accomplice? A dim jealousy stirred beneath Mrs. Peyton's other emotions: she was undergoing the agony which the mother feels at the first intrusion on her privilege of judging her child; and her voice had a flutter of resentment.

"You must have a poor opinion of his character," she said.

Miss Verney did not remove her eyes, but her blush deepened beautifully. "I have, at any rate," she Said, "a high one of his talent. I don't suppose many men have an equal amount of moral and intellectual energy."

"And you would cultivate the one at the expense of the other?"

"In certain cases, and up to a certain point." She shook out the long fur of her muff, one of those silvery flexible furs which clothe a woman with a delicate sumptuousness. Everything about her, at the moment, seemed rich and cold—everything, as Mrs. Peyton quickly noted, but the blush lingering under her dark skin; and so complete was the girl's self-command that the blush seemed to be there only because it had been forgotten.

"I dare say you think me strange," she continued. "Most people do, because I speak the truth. It's the easiest way of concealing one's feelings. I can, for instance, talk quite openly about Mr. Peyton under shelter of your inference that I shouldn't do so if I were what is called 'interested' in him. And as I am interested in him, my method has its advantages!" She ended with one of the fluttering laughs which seemed to flit from point to point of her expressive person.

Mrs. Peyton leaned toward her. "I believe you are interested," she said quietly; "and since I suppose you allow others the privilege you claim for yourself, I am going to confess that I followed you here in the hope of finding out the nature of your interest."

Miss Verney shot a glance at her, and drew away in a soft subsidence of undulating furs.

"Is this an embassy?" she asked smiling.

"No: not in any sense."

The girl leaned back with an air of relief. "I'm glad; I should have disliked—" She looked again at Mrs. Peyton. "You want to know what I mean to do?"

"Yes."

"Then I can only answer that I mean to wait and see what he does."

"You mean that everything is contingent on his success?"

"I am—if I'm everything," she admitted gaily.

The mother's heart was beating in her throat, and her words seemed to force themselves out through the throbs.

"I—I don't quite see why you attach such importance to this special success."

"Because he does," the girl returned instantly. "Because to him it is the final answer to his self-questioning, the questioning whether he is ever to amount to anything or not. He says if he has anything in him it ought to come out now. All the conditions are favourable, it is the chance he has always prayed for. You see," she continued, almost confidentially, but without the least loss of composure—"you see he has told me a great deal about himself and his various experiments, his phrases of indecision and disgust. There are lots of tentative talents in the world, and the sooner they are crushed out by circumstances the better. But it seems as though he really had it in him to do something distinguished, as though the uncertainty lay in his character and not in his talent. That is what interests, what attracts me. One can't teach a man to have genius, but if he has it one may show him how to use it. That is what I should be good for, you see, to keep him up to his opportunities."

Mrs. Peyton had listened with an intensity of attention that left her reply unprepared. There was something startling and yet half attractive in the girl's avowal of principles which are oftener lived by than professed.

"And you think," she began at length, "that in this case he has fallen below his opportunity?"

"No one can tell, of course; but his discouragement, his abatement, is a bad sign. I don't think he has any hope of succeeding."

The mother again wavered a moment. "Since you are so frank," she then said, "will you let me be equally so, and ask how lately you have seen him?"

The girl smiled at the circumlocution. "Yesterday afternoon," she said simply.

"And you thought him—"

"Horribly down on his luck. He said himself that his brain was empty."

Again Mrs. Peyton felt the throb in her throat, and a slow blush rose to her cheek. "Was that all he said?"

"About himself, was there anything else?" said the girl quickly.

"He didn't tell you of—of an opportunity to make up for the time he has lost?"

"An opportunity? I don't understand."

"He didn't speak to you, then, of Mr. Darrow's letter?"

"He said nothing of any letter."

"There was one, which was found after poor Darrow's death. In it he gave Dick leave to use his design for the competition. Dick says the design is wonderful, it would give him just what he needs."

Miss Verney sat listening raptly, with a rush of colour that suffused her like light.

"But when was this? Where was the letter found? He never said a word of it!" she exclaimed.

"The letter was found on the day of Darrow's death."

"But I don't understand! Why has he never told me? Why should he seem so hopeless?" She turned an ignorant appealing face on Mrs. Peyton. It was prodigious, but it was true, she felt nothing, saw nothing, but the crude fact of the opportunity.

Mrs. Peyton's voice trembled with the completeness of her triumph. "I suppose his reason for not speaking is that he has scruples."

"Scruples?"

"He feels that to use the design would be dishonest."

Miss Verney's eyes fixed themselves on her in a commiserating stare. "Dishonest? When the poor man wished it himself? When it was his last request? When the letter is there to prove it? Why, the design belongs to your son! No one else had any right to it."

"But Dick's right does not extend to passing it off as his own, at least that is his feeling, I believe. If he won the competition he would be winning it on false pretenses."

"Why should you call them false pretenses? His design might have been better than Darrow's if he had had time to carry it out. It seems to me that Mr. Darrow must have felt this, must have felt that he owed his friend some compensation for the time he took from him. I can imagine nothing more natural than his wishing to make this return for your son's sacrifice."

She positively glowed with the force of her conviction, and Mrs. Peyton, for a strange instant, felt her own resistance wavering. She herself had never considered the question in that light, the light of Darrow's viewing his gift as a justifiable compensation. But the glimpse she caught of it drove her shuddering behind her retrenchments.

"That argument," she said coldly, "would naturally be more convincing to Darrow than to my son."

Miss Verney glanced up, struck by the change in Mrs. Peyton's voice.

"Ah, then you agree with him? You think it would be dishonest?"

Mrs. Peyton saw that she had slipped into self-betrayal. "My son and I have not spoken of the matter," she said evasively. She caught the flash of relief in Miss Verney's face.

"You haven't spoken? Then how do you know how he feels about it?"

"I only judge from—well, perhaps from his not speaking."

The girl drew a deep breath. "I see," she murmured. "That is the very reason that prevents his speaking."

"The reason?"

"Your knowing what he thinks—and his knowing that you know."

Mrs. Peyton was startled at her subtlety. "I assure you," she said, rising, "that I have done nothing to influence him."

The girl gazed at her musingly. "No," she said with a faint smile, "nothing except to read his thoughts."

VI

Mrs. Peyton reached home in the state of exhaustion which follows on a physical struggle. It seemed to her as though her talk with Clemence Verney had been an actual combat, a measuring of wrist and eye. For a moment she was frightened at what she had done, she felt as though she had betrayed her son to the enemy. But before long she regained her moral balance, and saw that she had merely shifted the conflict to the ground on which it could best be fought out, since the prize fought for was the natural battlefield. The reaction brought with it a sense of helplessness, a realization that she had let the issue pass out of her hold; but since, in the last analysis, it had never lain there, since it was above all needful that the determining touch should be given by any hand but hers, she presently found courage to subside into inaction. She had done all she could, even more, perhaps, than prudence warranted, and now she could but await passively the working of the forces she had set in motion.

For two days after her talk with Miss Verney she saw little of Dick. He went early to his office and came back late. He seemed less tired, more self-possessed, than during the first days after Darrow's death; but there was a new inscrutableness in his manner, a note of reserve, of resistance almost, as though he had barricaded himself against her conjectures. She had been struck by Miss Verney's reply to the anxious asseveration that she had done nothing to influence Dick—"Nothing," the girl had answered, "except to read his thoughts." Mrs. Peyton shrank from this detection of a tacit interference with her son's liberty of action. She longed, how passionately he would never know, to stand apart from him in this struggle between his two destinies, and it was almost a relief that he on his side should hold aloof, should, for the first time in their relation, seem to feel her tenderness as an intrusion.

Only four days remained before the date fixed for the sending in of the designs, and still Dick had not referred to his work. Of Darrow, also, he had made no mention. His mother longed to know if he had spoken to Clemence Verney, or rather if the girl had forced his confidence. Mrs. Peyton was almost certain that Miss Verney would not remain silent, there were times when Dick's renewed application to his work seemed an earnest of her having spoken, and spoken convincingly. At the thought Kate's heart grew chill. What if her experiment should succeed in a sense she had not intended? If the girl should reconcile Dick to his weakness, should pluck the sting from his temptation? In this round of uncertainties the mother revolved for two interminable days; but the second evening brought an answer to her question.

Dick, returning earlier than usual from the office, had found, on the hall-table, a note which, since morning, had been under his mother's observation. The envelope, fashionable in tint and texture, was addressed in a rapid staccato hand which seemed the very imprint of Miss Verney's utterance. Mrs. Peyton did not know the girl's writing; but such notes had of late lain often enough on the hall-table to make their attribution easy. This communication Dick, as his mother poured his tea, looked over with a face of shifting lights; then he folded it into his note-case, and said, with a glance at his watch: "If you haven't asked any one for this evening I think I'll dine out."

"Do, dear; the change will be good for you," his mother assented.

He made no answer, but sat leaning back, his hands clasped behind his head, his eyes fixed on the fire. Every line of his body expressed a profound physical lassitude, but the face remained alert and guarded. Mrs. Peyton, in silence, was busying herself with the details of the tea-making, when suddenly, inexplicably, a question forced itself to her lips.

"And your work—?" she said, strangely hearing herself speak.

"My work—?" He sat up, on the defensive almost, but without a tremor of the guarded face.

"You're getting on well? You've made up for lost time?"

"Oh, yes: things are going better." He rose, with another glance at his watch. "Time to dress," he said, nodding to her as he turned to the door.

It was an hour later, during her own solitary dinner, that a ring at the door was followed by the parlour-maid's announcement that Mr. Gill was there from the office. In the hall, in fact, Kate found her son's partner, who explained apologetically that he had understood Peyton was dining at home, and had come to consult him about a difficulty which had arisen since he had left the office. On hearing that Dick was out, and that his mother did not know where he had gone, Mr. Gill's perplexity became so manifest that Mrs. Peyton, after a moment, said hesitatingly: "He may be at a friend's house; I could give you the address."

The architect caught up his hat. "Thank you; I'll have a try for him."

Mrs. Peyton hesitated again. "Perhaps," she suggested, "it would be better to telephone."

She led the way into the little study behind the drawing-room, where a telephone stood on the writing-table. The folding doors between the two rooms were open: should she close them as she passed back into the drawing-room? On the threshold she wavered an instant; then she walked on and took her usual seat by the fire.

Gill, meanwhile, at the telephone, had "rung up" the Verney house, and inquired if his partner were dining there. The reply was evidently affirmative; and a moment later Kate knew that he was in communication with her son. She sat motionless, her hands clasped on the arms of her chair, her head erect, in an attitude of avowed attention. If she listened she would listen openly: there should be no suspicion of eavesdropping. Gill, engrossed in his message, was probably hardly conscious of her presence; but if he turned his head he should at least have no difficulty in seeing her, and in being aware that she could hear what he said. Gill, however, as she was quick to remember, was doubtless ignorant of any need for secrecy in his communication to Dick. He had often heard the affairs of the office discussed openly before Mrs. Peyton, had been led to regard her as familiar with all the details of her son's work. He talked on unconcernedly, and she listened.

Ten minutes later, when he rose to go, she knew all that she had wanted to find out. Long familiarity with the technicalities of her son's profession made it easy for her to translate the stenographic jargon of the office. She could lengthen out all Gill's abbreviations, interpret all his allusions, and reconstruct Dick's answers from the questions addressed to him. And when the door closed on the architect she was left face to face with the fact that her son, unknown to any one but herself, was using Darrow's drawings to complete his work.

Mrs. Peyton, left alone, found it easier to continue her vigil by the drawing-room fire than to carry up to the darkness and silence of her own room the truth she had been at such pains to acquire. She had no thought of sitting up for Dick. Doubtless, his dinner over, he would rejoin Gill at the office, and prolong through, the night the task in which she now knew him to be engaged. But it was less lonely by the fire than in the wide-eyed darkness which awaited her upstairs. A mortal loneliness enveloped her. She felt as though she had fallen by the way, spent and broken in a struggle of which even its object had been unconscious. She had tried to deflect the natural course of events, she had sacrificed her personal happiness to a fantastic ideal of duty, and it was her punishment to be left alone with her failure, outside the normal current of human strivings and regrets.

She had no wish to see her son just then: she would have preferred to let the inner tumult subside, to repossess herself in this new adjustment to life, before meeting his eyes again. But as she sat there, far adrift on her misery, she was aroused by the turning of his key in the latch. She started up, her heart sounding a retreat, but her faculties too dispersed to obey it; and while she stood wavering, the door opened and he was in the room.

In the room, and with face illumined: a Dick she had not seen since the strain of the contest had cast its shade on him. Now he shone as in a sunrise of victory, holding out exultant hands from which she hung back instinctively.

"Mother! I knew you'd be waiting for me!" He had her on his breast now, and his kisses were in her hair. "I've always said you knew everything that was happening to me, and now you've guessed that I wanted you to-night."

She was struggling faintly against the dear endearments. "What has happened?" she murmured, drawing back for a dazzled look at him.

He had drawn her to the sofa, had dropped beside her, regaining his hold of her in the boyish need that his happiness should be touched and handled.

"My engagement has happened!" he cried out to her. "You stupid dear, do you need to be told?"

VII

She had indeed needed to be told: the surprise was complete and overwhelming. She sat silent under it, her hands trembling in his, till the blood mounted to his face and she felt his confident grasp relax.

"You didn't guess it, then?" he exclaimed, starting up and moving away from her.

"No; I didn't guess it," she confessed in a dead-level voice.

He stood above her, half challenging, half defensive. "And you haven't a word to say to me? Mother!" he adjured her.

She rose too, putting her arms about him with a kiss. "Dick! Dear Dick!" she murmured.

"She imagines you don't like her; she says she's always felt it. And yet she owns you've been delightful, that you've tried to make friends with her. And I thought you knew how much it would mean to me, just now, to have this uncertainty over, and that you'd actually been trying to help me, to put in a good word for me. I thought it was you who had made her decide."

"I?"

"By your talk with her the other day. She told me of your talk with her."

His mother's hands slipped from his shoulders and she sank back into her seat. She felt the cruelty of her silence, but only an inarticulate murmur found a way to her lips. Before speaking she must clear a space in the suffocating rush of her sensations. For the moment she could only repeat inwardly that Clemence Verney had yielded before the final test, and that she herself was somehow responsible for this fresh entanglement of fate. For she saw in a flash how the coils of circumstance had tightened; and as her mind cleared it was filled with the perception that this, precisely, was what the girl intended, that this was why she had conferred the crown before the victory. By pledging herself to Dick she had secured his pledge in return: had put him on his honour in a cynical inversion of the term. Kate saw the succession of events spread out before her like a map, and the astuteness of the girl's policy frightened her. Miss Verney had conducted the campaign like a strategist. She had frankly owned that her interest in Dick's future depended on his capacity for success, and in order to key him up to his first achievement she had given him a foretaste of its results.

So much was almost immediately clear to Mrs. Peyton; but in a moment her inferences had carried her a point farther. For it was now plain to her that Miss Verney had not risked so much without first trying to gain her point at less cost: that if she had had to give herself as a prize, it was because no other bribe had been sufficient. This then, as the mother saw with a throb of hope, meant that Dick, who since Darrow's death had held to his purpose unwaveringly, had been deflected from it by the first hint of Clemence Verney's connivance. Kate had not miscalculated: things had happened as she had foreseen. In the light of the girl's approval his act had taken an odious look. He had recoiled from it, and it was to revive his flagging courage that she had had to promise herself, to take him in the meshes of her surrender.

Kate, looking up, saw above her the young perplexity of her boy's face, the suspended happiness waiting to brim over. With a fresh touch of misery she said to herself that this was his hour, his one irrecoverable moment, and that she was darkening it by her silence. Her memory went back to the same hour in her own life: she could feel its heat in her pulses still. What right had she to stand in Dick's light? Who was she to decide between his code and hers? She put out her hand and drew him down to her.

"She'll be the making of me, you know, mother," he said, as they leaned together. "She'll put new life in me, she'll help me get my second wind. Her talk is like a fresh breeze blowing away the fog in my head. I never knew any one who saw so straight to the heart of things, who had such a grip on values. She goes straight up to life and catches hold of it, and you simply can't make her let go."

He got up and walked the length of the room; then he came back and stood smiling above his mother.

"You know you and I are rather complicated people," he said. "We're always walking around things to get new views of them, we're always rearranging the furniture. And somehow she simplifies life so tremendously." He dropped down beside her with a deprecating laugh. "Not that I mean, dear, that it hasn't been good for me to argue things out with myself, as you've taught me to—only the man who stops to talk is apt to get shoved aside nowadays, and I don't believe Milton's archangels would have had much success in active business."

He had begun in a strain of easy confidence, but as he went on she detected an effort to hold the note, she felt that his words were being poured out in a vain attempt to fill the silence which was deepening between them. She longed, in her turn, to pour something into that menacing void, to bridge it with a reconciling word or look; but her soul hung back, and she had to take refuge in a vague murmur of tenderness.

"My boy! My boy!" she repeated; and he sat beside her without speaking, their hand-clasp alone spanning the distance which had widened between their thoughts.

The engagement, as Kate subsequently learned, was not to be made known till later. Miss Verney had even stipulated that for the present there should be no recognition of it in her own family or in Dick's. She did not wish to interfere with his final work for the competition, and had made him promise, as he laughingly owned, that he would not see her again till the drawings were sent in. His mother noticed that he made no other allusion to his work; but when he bade her good-night he added that he might not see her the next morning, as he had to go to the office early. She took this as a hint that he wished to be left alone, and kept her room the next day till the closing door told her that he was out of the house.

She herself had waked early, and it seemed to her that the day was already old when she came downstairs. Never had the house appeared so empty. Even in Dick's longest absences something of his presence had always hung about the rooms: a fine dust of memories and associations, which wanted only the evocation of her thought to float into a palpable semblance of him. But now he seemed to have taken himself quite away, to have broken every fibre by which their lives had hung together. Where the sense of him had been there was only a deeper emptiness: she felt as if a strange man had gone out of her house.

She wandered from room to room, aimlessly, trying to adjust herself to their solitude. She had known such loneliness before, in the years when most women's hearts are fullest; but that was long ago, and the solitude had after all been less complete, because of the sense that it might still be filled. Her son had come: her life had brimmed over; but now the tide ebbed again, and she was left gazing over a bare stretch of wasted years. Wasted! There was the mortal pang, the stroke from which there was no healing. Her faith and hope had been marsh-lights luring her to the wilderness, her love a vain edifice reared on shifting ground.

In her round of the rooms she came at last to Dick's study upstairs. It was full of his boyhood: she could trace the history of his past in its quaint relics and survivals, in the school-books lingering on his crowded shelves, the school-photographs and college-trophies hung among his later treasures. All his successes and failures, his exaltations and inconsistencies, were recorded in the warm huddled heterogeneous room. Everywhere she saw the touch of her own hand, the vestiges of her own steps. It was she alone who held the clue to the labyrinth, who could thread a way through the confusions and contradictions of his past; and her soul rejected the thought that his future could ever escape from her. She dropped down into his shabby college armchair and hid her face in the papers on his desk.

The day dwelt in her memory as a long stretch of aimless hours: blind alleys of time that led up to a dead wall of inaction.

Toward afternoon she remembered that she had promised to dine out and go to the opera. At first she felt that the contact of life would be unendurable; then she shrank from shutting herself up with her misery. In the end she let herself drift passively on the current of events, going through the mechanical routine of the day without much consciousness of what was happening.

At twilight, as she sat in the drawing-room, the evening paper was brought in, and in glancing over it her eye fell on a paragraph which seemed printed in more vivid type than the rest. It was headed, The New Museum of Sculpture, and underneath she read: "The artists and architects selected to pass on the competitive designs for the new Museum will begin their sittings on Monday, and tomorrow is the last day on which designs may be sent in to the committee. Great interest is felt in the competition, as the conspicuous site chosen for the new building, and the exceptionally large sum voted by the city for its erection, offer an unusual field for the display of architectural ability."

She leaned back, closing her eyes. It was as though a clock had struck, loud and inexorably, marking off some irrecoverable hour. She was seized by a sudden longing to seek Dick out, to fall on her knees and plead with him: it was one of those physical obsessions against which the body has to stiffen its muscles as well as the mind its thoughts. Once she even sprang up to ring for a cab; but she sank back again, breathing as if after a struggle, and gripping the arms of her chair to keep herself down.

"I can only wait for him—only wait for him—" she heard herself say; and the words loosened the sobs in her throat.

At length she went upstairs to dress for dinner. A ghostlike self looked back at her from her toilet-glass: she watched it performing the mechanical gestures of the toilet, dressing her, as it appeared, without help from her actual self. Each little act stood out sharply against the blurred background of her brain: when she spoke to her maid her voice sounded extraordinarily loud. Never had the house been so silent; or, stay, yes, once she had felt the same silence, once when Dick, in his school-days, had been ill of a fever, and she had sat up with him on the decisive night. The silence had been as deep and as terrible then; and as she dressed she had before her the vision of his room, of the cot in which he lay, of his restless head working a hole in the pillow, his face so pinched and alien under the familiar freckles. It might be his death-watch she was keeping: the doctors had warned her to be ready. And in the silence her soul had fought for her boy, her love had hung over him like wings, her abundant useless hateful life had struggled to force itself into his empty veins. And she had succeeded, she had saved him, she had poured her life into him; and in place of the strange child she had watched all night, at daylight she held her own boy to her breast.

That night had once seemed to her the most dreadful of her life; but she knew now that it was one of the agonies which enrich, that the passion thus spent grows fourfold from its ashes. She could not have borne to keep this new vigil alone. She must escape from its sterile misery, must take refuge in other lives till she regained courage to face her own. At the opera, in the illumination of the first entr'acte, as she gazed about the house, wondering through the numb ache of her wretchedness how others could talk and smile and be indifferent, it seemed to her that all the jarring animation about her was suddenly focussed in the face of Clemence Verney. Miss Verney sat opposite, in the front of a crowded box, a box in which, continually, the black-coated background shifted and renewed itself. Mrs. Peyton felt a throb of anger at the girl's bright air of unconcern. She forgot that she too was talking, smiling, holding out her hand to newcomers, in a studied mimicry of life, while her real self played out its tragedy behind the scenes. Then it occurred to her that, to Clemence Verney, there was no tragedy in the situation. According to the girl's calculations, Dick was virtually certain of success; and unsuccess was to her the only conceivable disaster.

All through the opera the sense of that opposing force, that negation of her own beliefs, burned itself into Mrs. Peyton's consciousness. The space between herself and the girl seemed to vanish, the throng about them to disperse, till they were face to face and alone, enclosed in their mortal enmity. At length the feeling of humiliation and defeat grew unbearable to Mrs. Peyton. The girl seemed to flout her in the insolence of victory, to sit there as the visible symbol of her failure. It was better after all to be at home alone with her thoughts.

As she drove away from the opera she thought of that other vigil which, only a few streets away, Dick was perhaps still keeping. She wondered if his work were over, if the final stroke had been drawn. And as she pictured him there, signing his pact with evil in the loneliness of the conniving night, an uncontrollable impulse possessed her. She must drive by his windows and see if they were still alight. She would not go up to him, she dared not, but at least she would pass near to him, would invisibly share his watch and hover on the edge of his thoughts. She lowered the window and called out the address to the coachman.

The tall office-building loomed silent and dark as she approached it; but presently, high up, she caught a light in the familiar windows. Her heart gave a leap, and the light swam on her through tears. The carriage drew up, and for a moment she sat motionless. Then the coachman bent down toward her, and she saw that he was asking if he should drive on. She tried to shape a yes, but her lips refused it, and she shook her head. He continued to lean down perplexedly, and at length, under the interrogation of his attitude, it became impossible to sit still, and she opened the door and stepped out. It was equally impossible to stand on the sidewalk, and her next steps carried her to the door of the building. She groped for the bell and rang it, feeling still dimly accountable to the coachman for some consecutiveness of action, and after a moment the night watchman opened the door, drawing back amazed at the shining apparition which confronted him. Recognizing Mrs. Peyton, whom he had seen about the building by day, he tried to adapt himself to the situation by a vague stammer of apology.

"I came to see if my son is still here," she faltered.

"Yes, ma'am, he's here. He's been here most nights lately till after twelve."

"And is Mr. Gill with him?"

"No: Mr. Gill he went away just after I come on this evening."

She glanced up into the cavernous darkness of the stairs.

"Is he alone up there, do you think?"

"Yes, ma'am, I know he's alone, because I seen his men leaving soon after Mr. Gill."

Kate lifted her head quickly. "Then I will go up to him," she said.

The watchman apparently did not think it proper to offer any comment on this unusual proceeding, and a moment later she was fluttering and rustling up through the darkness, like a night-bird hovering among rafters. There were ten flights to climb: at every one her breath failed her, and she had to stand still and press her hands against her heart. Then the weight on her breast lifted, and she went on again, upward and upward, the great dark building dropping away from her, in tier after tier of mute doors and mysterious corridors. At last she reached Dick's floor, and saw the light shining down the passage from his door. She leaned against the wall, her breath coming short, the silence throbbing in her ears. Even now it was not too late to turn back. She bent over the stairs, letting her eyes plunge into the nether blackness, with the single glimmer of the watchman's lights in its depths; then she turned and stole toward her son's door.

There again she paused and listened, trying to catch, through the hum of her pulses, any noise that might come to her from within. But the silence was unbroken, it seemed as though the office must be empty. She pressed her ear to the door, straining for a sound. She knew he never sat long at his work, and it seemed unaccountable that she should not hear him moving about the drawing-board. For a moment she fancied he might be sleeping; but sleep did not come to him readily after prolonged mental effort, she recalled the restless straying of his feet above her head for hours after he returned from his night work in the office.

She began to fear that he might be ill. A nervous trembling seized her, and she laid her hand on the latch, whispering "Dick!"

Her whisper sounded loudly through the silence, but there was no answer, and after a pause she called again. With each call the hush seemed to deepen: it closed in on her, mysterious and impenetrable. Her heart was beating in short frightened leaps: a moment more and she would have cried out. She drew a quick breath and turned the door-handle.

The outer room, Dick's private office, with its red carpet and easy-chairs, stood in pleasant lamp-lit emptiness. The last time she had entered it, Darrow and Clemence Verney had been there, and she had sat behind the urn observing them. She paused a moment, struck now by a fault sound from beyond; then she slipped noiselessly across the carpet, pushed open the swinging door, and stood on the threshold of the work-room. Here the gas-lights hung a green-shaded circle of brightness over the great draughting-table in the middle of the floor. Table and floor were strewn with a confusion of papers, torn blue-prints and tracings, crumpled sheets of tracing-paper wrenched from the draughting-boards in a sudden fury of destruction; and in the centre of the havoc, his arms stretched across the table and his face hidden in them, sat Dick Peyton.

He did not seem to hear his mother's approach, and she stood looking at him, her breast tightening with a new fear.

"Dick!" she said, "Dick!—" and he sprang up, staring with dazed eyes. But gradually, as his gaze cleared, a light spread in it, a mounting brightness of recognition.

"You've come—you've come—" he said, stretching his hands to her; and all at once she had him in her breast as in a shelter.

"You wanted me?" she whispered as she held him.

He looked up at her, tired, breathless, with the white radiance of the runner near the goal.

"I had you, dear!" he said, smiling strangely on her; and her heart gave a great leap of understanding.

Her arms had slipped from his neck, and she stood leaning on him, deep-suffused in the shyness of her discovery. For it might still be that he did not wish her to know what she had done for him.

But he put his arm about her, boyishly, and drew her toward one of the hard seats between the tables; and there, on the bare floor, he knelt before her, and hid his face in her lap. She sat motionless, feeling the dear warmth of his head against her knees, letting her hands stray in faint caresses through his hair.

Neither spoke for awhile; then he raised his head and looked at her. "I suppose you know what has been happening to me," he said.

She shrank from seeming to press into his life a hair's-breadth farther than he was prepared to have her go. Her eyes turned from him toward the scattered drawings on the table.

"You have given up the competition?" she said.

"Yes, and a lot more." He stood up, the wave of emotion ebbing, yet leaving him nearer, in his recovered calmness, than in the shock of their first moment.

"I didn't know, at first, how much you guessed," he went on quietly. "I was sorry I'd shown you Darrow's letter; but it didn't worry me much because I didn't suppose you'd think it possible that I should, take advantage of it. It's only lately that I've understood that you knew everything." He looked at her with a smile. "I don't know yet how I found it out, for you're wonderful about keeping things to yourself, and you never made a sign. I simply felt it in a kind of nearness, as if I couldn't get away from you. Oh, there were times when I should have preferred not having you about, when I tried to turn my back on you, to see things from other people's standpoint. But you were always there, you wouldn't be discouraged. And I got tired of trying to explain things to you, of trying to bring you round to my way of thinking. You wouldn't go away and you wouldn't come any nearer, you just stood there and watched everything that I was doing."

He broke off, taking one of his restless turns down the long room. Then he drew up a chair beside her, and dropped into it with a great sigh.

"At first, you know, I hated it most awfully. I wanted to be let alone and to work out my own theory of things. If you'd said a word, if you'd tried to influence me, the spell would have been broken. But just because the actual you kept apart and didn't meddle or pry, the other, the you in my heart, seemed to get a tighter hold on me. I don't know how to tell you, it's all mixed up in my head—but old things you'd said and done kept coming back to me, crowding between me and what I was trying for, looking at me without speaking, like old friends I'd gone back on, till I simply couldn't stand it any longer. I fought it off till to-night, but when I came back to finish the work there you were again—and suddenly, I don't know how, you weren't an obstacle any longer, but a refuge—and I crawled into your arms as I used to when things went against me at school."

His hands stole back into hers, and he leaned his head against her shoulder like a boy.

"I'm an abysmally weak fool, you know," he ended; "I'm not worth the fight you've put up for me. But I want you to know that it's your doing, that if you had let go an instant I should have gone under—and that if I'd gone under I should never have come up again alive."

BUNNER SISTERS

PART I

I

In the days when New York's traffic moved at the pace of the drooping horse-car, when society applauded Christine Nilsson at the Academy of Music and basked in the sunsets of the Hudson River School on the walls of the National Academy of Design, an inconspicuous shop with a single show-window was intimately and favourably known to the feminine population of the quarter bordering on Stuyvesant Square.

It was a very small shop, in a shabby basement, in a side-street already doomed to decline; and from the miscellaneous display behind the window-pane, and the brevity of the sign surmounting it (merely "Bunner Sisters" in blotchy gold on a black ground) it would have been difficult for the uninitiated to guess the precise nature of the business carried on within. But that was of little consequence, since its fame was so purely local that the customers on whom its existence depended were almost congenitally aware of the exact range of "goods" to be found at Bunner Sisters'.

The house of which Bunner Sisters had annexed the basement was a private dwelling with a brick front, green shutters on weak hinges, and a dress-maker's sign in the window above the shop. On each side of its modest three stories stood higher buildings, with fronts of brown stone, cracked and blistered, cast-iron balconies and cat-haunted grass-patches behind twisted railings. These houses too had once been private, but now a cheap lunchroom filled the basement of one, while the other announced itself, above the knotty wistaria that clasped its central balcony, as the Mendoza Family Hotel. It was obvious from the chronic cluster of refuse-barrels at its area-gate and the blurred surface of its curtainless windows, that the families frequenting the Mendoza Hotel were not exacting in their tastes; though they doubtless indulged in as much fastidiousness as they could afford to pay for, and rather more than their landlord thought they had a right to express.

These three houses fairly exemplified the general character of the street, which, as it stretched eastward, rapidly fell from shabbiness to squalor, with an increasing frequency of projecting sign-boards, and of swinging doors that softly shut or opened at the touch of red-nosed men and pale little girls with broken jugs. The middle of the street was full of irregular depressions, well adapted to retain the long swirls of dust and straw and twisted paper that the wind drove up and down its sad untended length; and toward the end of the day, when traffic had been active, the fissured pavement formed a mosaic of coloured hand-bills, lids of tomato-cans, old shoes, cigar-stumps and banana skins, cemented together by a layer of mud, or veiled in a powdering of dust, as the state of the weather determined.

The sole refuge offered from the contemplation of this depressing waste was the sight of the Bunner Sisters' window. Its panes were always well-washed, and though their display of artificial flowers, bands of scalloped flannel, wire hat-frames, and jars of home-made preserves, had the undefinable greyish tinge of objects long preserved in the show-case of a museum, the window revealed a background of orderly counters and white-washed walls in pleasant contrast to the adjoining dinginess.

The Bunner sisters were proud of the neatness of their shop and content with its humble prosperity. It was not what they had once imagined it would be, but though it presented but a shrunken image of their earlier ambitions it enabled them to pay their rent and keep themselves alive and out of debt; and it was long since their hopes had soared higher.

Now and then, however, among their greyer hours there came one not bright enough to be called sunny, but rather of the silvery twilight hue which sometimes ends a day of storm. It was such an hour that Ann Eliza, the elder of the firm, was soberly enjoying as she sat one January evening in the back room which served as bedroom, kitchen and parlour to herself and her sister Evelina. In the shop the blinds had been drawn down, the counters cleared and the wares in the window lightly covered with an old sheet; but the shop-door remained unlocked till Evelina, who had taken a parcel to the dyer's, should come back.

In the back room a kettle bubbled on the stove, and Ann Eliza had laid a cloth over one end of the centre table, and placed near the green-shaded sewing lamp two tea-cups, two plates, a sugar-bowl and a piece of pie. The rest of the room remained in a greenish shadow which discreetly veiled the outline of an old-fashioned mahogany bedstead surmounted by a chromo of a young lady in a night-gown who clung with eloquently-rolling eyes to a crag described in illuminated letters as the Rock of Ages; and against the unshaded windows two rocking-chairs and a sewing-machine were silhouetted on the dusk.

Ann Eliza, her small and habitually anxious face smoothed to unusual serenity, and the streaks of pale hair on her veined temples shining glossily beneath the lamp, had seated herself at the table, and was tying up, with her usual fumbling deliberation, a knobby object wrapped in paper. Now and then, as she struggled with the string, which was too short, she fancied she heard the click of the shop-door, and paused to listen for her sister; then, as no one came, she straightened her spectacles and entered into renewed conflict with the parcel. In honour of some event of obvious importance, she had put on her double-dyed and triple-turned black silk. Age, while bestowing on this garment a patine worthy of a Renaissance bronze, had deprived it of whatever curves the wearer's pre-Raphaelite figure had once been able to impress on it; but this stiffness of outline gave it an air of sacerdotal state which seemed to emphasize the importance of the occasion.

Seen thus, in her sacramental black silk, a wisp of lace turned over the collar and fastened by a mosaic brooch, and her face smoothed into harmony with her apparel, Ann Eliza looked ten years younger than behind the counter, in the heat and burden of the day. It would have been as difficult to guess her approximate age as that of the black silk, for she had the same worn and glossy aspect as her dress; but a faint tinge of pink still lingered on her cheek-bones, like the reflection of sunset which sometimes colours the west long after the day is over.

When she had tied the parcel to her satisfaction, and laid it with furtive accuracy just opposite her sister's plate, she sat down, with an air of obviously-assumed indifference, in one of the rocking-chairs near the window; and a moment later the shop-door opened and Evelina entered.

The younger Bunner sister, who was a little taller than her elder, had a more pronounced nose, but a weaker slope of mouth and chin. She still permitted herself the frivolity of waving her pale hair, and its tight little ridges, stiff as the tresses of an Assyrian statue, were flattened under a dotted veil which ended at the tip of her cold-reddened nose. In her scant jacket and skirt of black cashmere she looked singularly nipped and faded; but it seemed possible that under happier conditions she might still warm into relative youth.

"Why, Ann Eliza," she exclaimed, in a thin voice pitched to chronic fretfulness, "what in the world you got your best silk on for?"

Ann Eliza had risen with a blush that made her steel-browed spectacles incongruous.

"Why, Evelina, why shouldn't I, I sh'ld like to know? Ain't it your birthday, dear?" She put out her arms with the awkwardness of habitually repressed emotion.

Evelina, without seeming to notice the gesture, threw back the jacket from her narrow shoulders.

"Oh, pshaw," she said, less peevishly. "I guess we'd better give up birthdays. Much as we can do to keep Christmas nowadays."

"You hadn't oughter say that, Evelina. We ain't so badly off as all that. I guess you're cold and tired. Set down while I take the kettle off: it's right on the boil."

She pushed Evelina toward the table, keeping a sideward eye on her sister's listless movements, while her own hands were busy with the kettle. A moment later came the exclamation for which she waited.

"Why, Ann Eliza!" Evelina stood transfixed by the sight of the parcel beside her plate.

Ann Eliza, tremulously engaged in filling the teapot, lifted a look of hypocritical surprise.

"Sakes, Evelina! What's the matter?"

The younger sister had rapidly untied the string, and drawn from its wrappings a round nickel clock of the kind to be bought for a dollar-seventy-five.

"Oh, Ann Eliza, how could you?" She set the clock down, and the sisters exchanged agitated glances across the table.

"Well," the elder retorted, "AIN'T it your birthday?"

"Yes, but—"

"Well, and ain't you had to run round the corner to the Square every morning, rain or shine, to see what time it was, ever since we had to sell mother's watch last July? Ain't you, Evelina?"

"Yes, but—"

"There ain't any buts. We've always wanted a clock and now we've got one: that's all there is about it. Ain't she a beauty, Evelina?" Ann Eliza, putting back the kettle on the stove, leaned over her sister's shoulder to pass an approving hand over the circular rim of the clock. "Hear how loud she ticks. I was afraid you'd hear her soon as you come in."

"No. I wasn't thinking," murmured Evelina.

"Well, ain't you glad now?" Ann Eliza gently reproached her. The rebuke had no acerbity, for she knew that Evelina's seeming indifference was alive with unexpressed scruples.

"I'm real glad, sister; but you hadn't oughter. We could have got on well enough without."

"Evelina Bunner, just you sit down to your tea. I guess I know what I'd oughter and what I'd hadn't oughter just as well as you do—I'm old enough!"

"You're real good, Ann Eliza; but I know you've given up something you needed to get me this clock."

"What do I need, I'd like to know? Ain't I got a best black silk?" the elder sister said with a laugh full of nervous pleasure.

She poured out Evelina's tea, adding some condensed milk from the jug, and cutting for her the largest slice of pie; then she drew up her own chair to the table.

The two women ate in silence for a few moments before Evelina began to speak again. "The clock is perfectly lovely and I don't say it ain't a comfort to have it; but I hate to think what it must have cost you."

"No, it didn't, neither," Ann Eliza retorted. "I got it dirt cheap, if you want to know. And I paid for it out of a little extra work I did the other night on the machine for Mrs. Hawkins."

"The baby-waists?"

"Yes."

"There, I knew it! You swore to me you'd buy a new pair of shoes with that money."

"Well, and s'posin' I didn't want 'em, what then? I've patched up the old ones as good as new, and I do declare, Evelina Bunner, if you ask me another question you'll go and spoil all my pleasure."

"Very well, I won't," said the younger sister.

They continued to eat without farther words. Evelina yielded to her sister's entreaty that she should finish the pie, and poured out a second cup of tea, into which she put the last lump of sugar; and between them, on the table, the clock kept up its sociable tick.

"Where'd you get it, Ann Eliza?" asked Evelina, fascinated.

"Where'd you s'pose? Why, right round here, over acrost the Square, in the queerest little store you ever laid eyes on. I saw it in the window as I was passing, and I stepped right in and asked how much it was, and the store-keeper he was real pleasant about it. He was just the nicest man. I guess he's a German. I told him I couldn't give much, and he said, well, he knew what hard times was too. His name's Ramy, Herman Ramy: I saw it written up over the store. And he told me he used to work at Tiff'ny's, oh, for years, in the clock-department, and three years ago he took sick with some kinder fever, and lost his place, and when he got well they'd engaged somebody else and didn't want him, and so he started this little store by himself. I guess he's real smart, and he spoke quite like an educated man, but he looks sick."

Evelina was listening with absorbed attention. In the narrow lives of the two sisters such an episode was not to be under-rated.

"What you say his name was?" she asked as Ann Eliza paused.

"Herman Ramy."

"How old is he?"

"Well, I couldn't exactly tell you, he looked so sick, but I don't b'lieve he's much over forty."

By this time the plates had been cleared and the teapot emptied, and the two sisters rose from the table. Ann Eliza, tying an apron over her black silk, carefully removed all traces of the meal; then, after washing the cups and plates, and putting them away in a cupboard, she drew her rocking-chair to the lamp and sat down to a heap of mending. Evelina, meanwhile, had been roaming about the room in search of an abiding-place for the clock. A rosewood what-not with ornamental fret-work hung on the wall beside the devout young lady in dishabille, and after much weighing of alternatives the sisters decided to dethrone a broken china vase filled with dried grasses which had long stood on the top shelf, and to put the clock in its place; the vase, after farther consideration, being relegated to a small table covered with blue and white beadwork, which held a Bible and prayer-book, and an illustrated copy of Longfellow's poems given as a school-prize to their father.

This change having been made, and the effect studied from every angle of the room, Evelina languidly put her pinking-machine on the table, and sat down to the monotonous work of pinking a heap of black silk flounces. The strips of stuff slid slowly to the floor at her side, and the clock, from its commanding altitude, kept time with the dispiriting click of the instrument under her fingers.

II

The purchase of Evelina's clock had been a more important event in the life of Ann Eliza Bunner than her younger sister could divine. In the first place, there had been the demoralizing satisfaction of finding herself in possession of a sum of money which she need not put into the common fund, but could spend as she chose, without consulting Evelina, and then the excitement of her stealthy trips abroad, undertaken on the rare occasions when she could trump up a pretext for leaving the shop; since, as a rule, it was Evelina who took the bundles to the dyer's, and delivered the purchases of those among their customers who were too genteel to be seen carrying home a bonnet or a bundle of pinking, so that, had it not been for the excuse of having to see Mrs. Hawkins's teething baby, Ann Eliza would hardly have known what motive to allege for deserting her usual seat behind the counter.

The infrequency of her walks made them the chief events of her life. The mere act of going out from the monastic quiet of the shop into the tumult of the streets filled her with a subdued excitement which grew too intense for pleasure as she was swallowed by the engulfing roar of Broadway or Third Avenue, and began to do timid battle with their incessant cross-currents of humanity. After a glance or two into the great show-windows she usually allowed herself to be swept back into the shelter of a side-street, and finally regained her own roof in a state of breathless bewilderment and fatigue; but gradually, as her nerves were soothed by the familiar quiet of the little shop, and the click of Evelina's pinking-machine, certain sights and sounds would detach themselves from the torrent along which she had been swept, and she would devote the rest of the day to a mental reconstruction of the different episodes of her walk, till finally it took shape in her thought as a consecutive and highly-coloured experience, from which, for weeks afterwards, she would detach some fragmentary recollection in the course of her long dialogues with her sister.

But when, to the unwonted excitement of going out, was added the intenser interest of looking for a present for Evelina, Ann Eliza's agitation, sharpened by concealment, actually preyed upon her rest; and it was not till the present had been given, and she had unbosomed herself of the experiences connected with its purchase, that she could look back with anything like composure to that stirring moment of her life. From that day forward, however, she began to take a certain tranquil pleasure in thinking of Mr. Ramy's small shop, not unlike her own in its countrified obscurity, though the layer of dust which covered its counter and shelves made the comparison only superficially acceptable. Still, she did not judge the state of the shop severely, for Mr. Ramy had told her that he was alone in the world, and lone men, she was aware, did not know how to deal with dust. It gave her a good deal of occupation to wonder why he had never married, or if, on the other hand, he were a widower, and had lost all his dear little children; and she scarcely knew which alternative seemed to make him the more interesting. In either case, his life was assuredly a sad one; and she passed many hours in speculating on the manner in which he probably spent his evenings. She knew he lived at the back of his shop, for she had caught, on entering, a glimpse of a dingy room with a tumbled bed; and the pervading smell of cold fry suggested that he probably did his own cooking. She wondered if he did not often make his tea with water that had not boiled, and asked herself, almost jealously, who looked after the shop while he went to market. Then it occurred to her as likely that he bought his provisions at the same market as Evelina; and she was fascinated by the thought that he and her sister might constantly be meeting in total unconsciousness of the link between them. Whenever she reached this stage in her reflexions she lifted a furtive glance to the clock, whose loud staccato tick was becoming a part of her inmost being.

The seed sown by these long hours of meditation germinated at last in the secret wish to go to market some morning in Evelina's stead. As this purpose rose to the surface of Ann Eliza's thoughts she shrank back shyly from its contemplation. A plan so steeped in duplicity had never before taken shape in her crystalline soul. How was it possible for her to consider such a step? And, besides, (she did not possess sufficient logic to mark the downward trend of this "besides"), what excuse could she make that would not excite her sister's curiosity? From this second query it was an easy descent to the third: how soon could she manage to go?

It was Evelina herself, who furnished the necessary pretext by awaking with a sore throat on the day when she usually went to market. It was a Saturday, and as they always had their bit of steak on Sunday the expedition could not be postponed, and it seemed natural that Ann Eliza, as she tied an old stocking around Evelina's throat, should announce her intention of stepping round to the butcher's.

"Oh, Ann Eliza, they'll cheat you so," her sister wailed.

Ann Eliza brushed aside the imputation with a smile, and a few minutes later, having set the room to rights, and cast a last glance at the shop, she was tying on her bonnet with fumbling haste.

The morning was damp and cold, with a sky full of sulky clouds that would not make room for the sun, but as yet dropped only an occasional snow-flake. In the early light the street looked its meanest and most neglected; but to Ann Eliza, never greatly troubled by any untidiness for which she was not responsible, it seemed to wear a singularly friendly aspect.

A few minutes' walk brought her to the market where Evelina made her purchases, and where, if he had any sense of topographical fitness, Mr. Ramy must also deal.

Ann Eliza, making her way through the outskirts of potato-barrels and flabby fish, found no one in the shop but the gory-aproned butcher who stood in the background cutting chops.

As she approached him across the tesselation of fish-scales, blood and saw-dust, he laid aside his cleaver and not unsympathetically asked: "Sister sick?"

"Oh, not very, jest a cold," she answered, as guiltily as if Evelina's illness had been feigned. "We want a steak as usual, please, and my sister said you was to be sure to give me jest as good a cut as if it was her," she added with child-like candour.

"Oh, that's all right." The butcher picked up his weapon with a grin. "Your sister knows a cut as well as any of us," he remarked.

In another moment, Ann Eliza reflected, the steak would be cut and wrapped up, and no choice left her but to turn her disappointed steps toward home. She was too shy to try to delay the butcher by such conversational arts as she possessed, but the approach of a deaf old lady in an antiquated bonnet and mantle gave her her opportunity.

"Wait on her first, please," Ann Eliza whispered. "I ain't in any hurry."

The butcher advanced to his new customer, and Ann Eliza, palpitating in the back of the shop, saw that the old lady's hesitations between liver and pork chops were likely to be indefinitely prolonged. They were still unresolved when she was interrupted by the entrance of a blowsy Irish girl with a basket on her arm. The newcomer caused a momentary diversion, and when she had departed the old lady, who was evidently as intolerant of interruption as a professional story-teller, insisted on returning to the beginning of her complicated order, and weighing anew, with an anxious appeal to the butcher's arbitration, the relative advantages of pork and liver. But even her hesitations, and the intrusion on them of two or three other customers, were of no avail, for Mr. Ramy was not among those who entered the shop; and at last Ann Eliza, ashamed of staying longer, reluctantly claimed her steak, and walked home through the thickening snow.

Even to her simple judgment the vanity of her hopes was plain, and in the clear light that disappointment turns upon our actions she wondered how she could have been foolish enough to suppose that, even if Mr. Ramy DID go to that particular market, he would hit on the same day and hour as herself.

There followed a colourless week unmarked by farther incident. The old stocking cured Evelina's throat, and Mrs. Hawkins dropped in once or twice to talk of her baby's teeth; some new orders for pinking were received, and Evelina sold a bonnet to the lady with puffed sleeves. The lady with puffed sleeves, a resident of "the Square," whose name they had never learned, because she always carried her own parcels home, was the most distinguished and interesting figure on their horizon. She was youngish, she was elegant (as the title they had given her implied), and she had a sweet sad smile about which they had woven many histories; but even the news of her return to town, it was her first apparition that year, failed to arouse Ann Eliza's interest. All the small daily happenings which had once sufficed to fill the hours now appeared to her in their deadly insignificance; and for the first time in her long years of drudgery she rebelled at the dullness of her life. With Evelina such fits of discontent were habitual and openly proclaimed, and Ann Eliza still excused them as one of the prerogatives of youth. Besides, Evelina had not been intended by Providence to pine in such a narrow life: in the original plan of things, she had been meant to marry and have a baby, to wear silk on Sundays, and take a leading part in a Church circle. Hitherto opportunity had played her false;

and for all her superior aspirations and carefully crimped hair she had remained as obscure and unsought as Ann Eliza. But the elder sister, who had long since accepted her own fate, had never accepted Evelina's. Once a pleasant young man who taught in Sunday-school had paid the younger Miss Bunner a few shy visits. That was years since, and he had speedily vanished from their view. Whether he had carried with him any of Evelina's illusions, Ann Eliza had never discovered; but his attentions had clad her sister in a halo of exquisite possibilities.

Ann Eliza, in those days, had never dreamed of allowing herself the luxury of self-pity: it seemed as much a personal right of Evelina's as her elaborately crinkled hair. But now she began to transfer to herself a portion of the sympathy she had so long bestowed on Evelina. She had at last recognized her right to set up some lost opportunities of her own; and once that dangerous precedent established, they began to crowd upon her memory.

It was at this stage of Ann Eliza's transformation that Evelina, looking up one evening from her work, said suddenly: "My! She's stopped."

Ann Eliza, raising her eyes from a brown merino seam, followed her sister's glance across the room. It was a Monday, and they always wound the clock on Sundays.

"Are you sure you wound her yesterday, Evelina?"

"Jest as sure as I live. She must be broke. I'll go and see."

Evelina laid down the hat she was trimming, and took the clock from its shelf.

"There—I knew it! She's wound jest as TIGHT—what you suppose's happened to her, Ann Eliza?"

"I dunno, I'm sure," said the elder sister, wiping her spectacles before proceeding to a close examination of the clock.

With anxiously bent heads the two women shook and turned it, as though they were trying to revive a living thing; but it remained unresponsive to their touch, and at length Evelina laid it down with a sigh.

"Seems like somethin' DEAD, don't it, Ann Eliza? How still the room is!"

"Yes, ain't it?"

"Well, I'll put her back where she belongs," Evelina continued, in the tone of one about to perform the last offices for the departed. "And I guess," she added, "you'll have to step round to Mr. Ramy's to-morrow, and see if he can fix her."

Ann Eliza's face burned. "I—yes, I guess I'll have to," she stammered, stooping to pick up a spool of cotton which had rolled to the floor. A sudden heart-throb stretched the seams of her flat alpaca bosom, and a pulse leapt to life in each of her temples.

That night, long after Evelina slept, Ann Eliza lay awake in the unfamiliar silence, more acutely conscious of the nearness of the crippled clock than when it had volubly told out the minutes. The next morning she woke from a troubled dream of having carried it to Mr. Ramy's, and found that he and his shop had vanished; and all through the day's occupations the memory of this dream oppressed her.

It had been agreed that Ann Eliza should take the clock to be repaired as soon as they had dined; but while they were still at table a weak-eyed little girl in a black apron stabbed with innumerable pins burst in on them with the cry: "Oh, Miss Bunner, for mercy's sake! Miss Mellins has been took again."

Miss Mellins was the dress-maker upstairs, and the weak-eyed child one of her youthful apprentices.

Ann Eliza started from her seat. "I'll come at once. Quick, Evelina, the cordial!"

By this euphemistic name the sisters designated a bottle of cherry brandy, the last of a dozen inherited from their grandmother, which they kept locked in their cupboard against such emergencies. A moment later, cordial in hand, Ann Eliza was hurrying upstairs behind the weak-eyed child.

Miss Mellins' "turn" was sufficiently serious to detain Ann Eliza for nearly two hours, and dusk had fallen when she took up the depleted bottle of cordial and descended again to the shop. It was empty, as usual, and Evelina sat at her pinking-machine in the back room. Ann Eliza was still agitated by her efforts to restore the dress-maker, but in spite of her preoccupation she was struck, as soon as she entered, by the loud tick of the clock, which still stood on the shelf where she had left it.

"Why, she's going!" she gasped, before Evelina could question her about Miss Mellins. "Did she start up again by herself?"

"Oh, no; but I couldn't stand not knowing what time it was, I've got so accustomed to having her round; and just after you went upstairs Mrs. Hawkins dropped in, so I asked her to tend the store for a minute, and I clapped on my things and ran right round to Mr. Ramy's. It turned out there wasn't anything the matter with her, nothin' on'y a speck of dust in the works, and he fixed her for me in a minute and I brought her right back. Ain't it lovely to hear her going again? But tell me about Miss Mellins, quick!"

For a moment Ann Eliza found no words. Not till she learned that she had missed her chance did she understand how many hopes had hung upon it. Even now she did not know why she had wanted so much to see the clock-maker again.

"I s'pose it's because nothing's ever happened to me," she thought, with a twinge of envy for the fate which gave Evelina every opportunity that came their way. "She had the Sunday-school teacher too," Ann Eliza murmured to herself; but she was well-trained in the arts of renunciation, and after a scarcely perceptible pause she plunged into a detailed description of the dress-maker's "turn."

Evelina, when her curiosity was roused, was an insatiable questioner, and it was supper-time before she had come to the end of her enquiries about Miss Mellins; but when the two sisters had seated themselves at their evening meal Ann Eliza at last found a chance to say: "So she on'y had a speck of dust in her."

Evelina understood at once that the reference was not to Miss Mellins. "Yes, at least he thinks so," she answered, helping herself as a matter of course to the first cup of tea.

"On'y to think!" murmured Ann Eliza.

"But he isn't SURE," Evelina continued, absently pushing the teapot toward her sister. "It may be something wrong with the—I forget what he called it. Anyhow, he said he'd call round and see, day after to-morrow, after supper."

"Who said?" gasped Ann Eliza.

"Why, Mr. Ramy, of course. I think he's real nice, Ann Eliza. And I don't believe he's forty; but he DOES look sick. I guess he's pretty lonesome, all by himself in that store. He as much as told me so, and somehow"—Evelina paused and bridled—"I kinder thought that maybe his saying he'd call round about the clock was on'y just an excuse. He said it just as I was going out of the store. What you think, Ann Eliza?"

"Oh, I don't har'ly know." To save herself, Ann Eliza could produce nothing warmer.

"Well, I don't pretend to be smarter than other folks," said Evelina, putting a conscious hand to her hair, "but I guess Mr. Herman Ramy wouldn't be sorry to pass an evening here, 'stead of spending it all alone in that poky little place of his."

Her self-consciousness irritated Ann Eliza.

"I guess he's got plenty of friends of his own," she said, almost harshly.

"No, he ain't, either. He's got hardly any."

"Did he tell you that too?" Even to her own ears there was a faint sneer in the interrogation.

"Yes, he did," said Evelina, dropping her lids with a smile. "He seemed to be just crazy to talk to somebody, somebody agreeable, I mean. I think the man's unhappy, Ann Eliza."

"So do I," broke from the elder sister.

"He seems such an educated man, too. He was reading the paper when I went in. Ain't it sad to think of his being reduced to that little store, after being years at Tiff'ny's, and one of the head men in their clock-department?"

"He told you all that?"

"Why, yes. I think he'd a' told me everything ever happened to him if I'd had the time to stay and listen. I tell you he's dead lonely, Ann Eliza."

"Yes," said Ann Eliza.

III

Two days afterward, Ann Eliza noticed that Evelina, before they sat down to supper, pinned a crimson bow under her collar; and when the meal was finished the younger sister, who seldom concerned herself with the clearing of the table, set about with nervous haste to help Ann Eliza in the removal of the dishes.

"I hate to see food mussing about," she grumbled. "Ain't it hateful having to do everything in one room?"

"Oh, Evelina, I've always thought we was so comfortable," Ann Eliza protested.

"Well, so we are, comfortable enough; but I don't suppose there's any harm in my saying I wisht we had a parlour, is there? Anyway, we might manage to buy a screen to hide the bed."

Ann Eliza coloured. There was something vaguely embarrassing in Evelina's suggestion.

"I always think if we ask for more what we have may be taken from us," she ventured.

"Well, whoever took it wouldn't get much," Evelina retorted with a laugh as she swept up the table-cloth.

A few moments later the back room was in its usual flawless order and the two sisters had seated themselves near the lamp. Ann Eliza had taken up her sewing, and Evelina was preparing to make artificial flowers. The sisters usually relegated this more delicate business to the long leisure of the summer months; but to-night Evelina had brought out the box which lay all winter under the bed, and spread before her a bright array of muslin petals, yellow stamens and green corollas, and a tray of little implements curiously suggestive of the dental art. Ann Eliza made no remark on this unusual proceeding; perhaps she guessed why, for that evening her sister had chosen a graceful task.

Presently a knock on the outer door made them look up; but Evelina, the first on her feet, said promptly: "Sit still. I'll see who it is."

Ann Eliza was glad to sit still: the baby's petticoat that she was stitching shook in her fingers.

"Sister, here's Mr. Ramy come to look at the clock," said Evelina, a moment later, in the high drawl she cultivated before strangers; and a shortish man with a pale bearded face and upturned coat-collar came stiffly into the room.

Ann Eliza let her work fall as she stood up. "You're very welcome, I'm sure, Mr. Ramy. It's real kind of you to call."

"Nod ad all, ma'am." A tendency to illustrate Grimm's law in the interchange of his consonants betrayed the clockmaker's nationality, but he was evidently used to speaking English, or at least the particular branch of the vernacular with which the Bunner sisters were familiar. "I don't like to led any clock go out of my store without being sure it gives satisfaction," he added.

"Oh, but we were satisfied," Ann Eliza assured him.

"But I wasn't, you see, ma'am," said Mr. Ramy looking slowly about the room, "nor I won't be, not till I see that clock's going all right."

"May I assist you off with your coat, Mr. Ramy?" Evelina interposed. She could never trust Ann Eliza to remember these opening ceremonies.

"Thank you, ma'am," he replied, and taking his thread-bare over-coat and shabby hat she laid them on a chair with the gesture she imagined the lady with the puffed sleeves might make use of on similar occasions. Ann Eliza's social sense was roused, and she felt that the next act of hospitality must be hers. "Won't you suit yourself to a seat?" she suggested. "My sister will reach down the clock; but I'm sure she's all right again. She's went beautiful ever since you fixed her."

"Dat's good," said Mr. Ramy. His lips parted in a smile which showed a row of yellowish teeth with one or two gaps in it; but in spite of this disclosure Ann Eliza thought his smile extremely pleasant: there was something wistful and conciliating in it which agreed with the pathos of his sunken cheeks and prominent eyes. As he took the lamp, the light fell on his bulging forehead and wide skull thinly covered with grayish hair. His hands were pale and broad, with knotty joints and square finger-tips rimmed with grime; but his touch was as light as a woman's.

"Well, ladies, dat clock's all right," he pronounced.

"I'm sure we're very much obliged to you," said Evelina, throwing a glance at her sister.

"Oh," Ann Eliza murmured, involuntarily answering the admonition. She selected a key from the bunch that hung at her waist with her cutting-out scissors, and fitting it into the lock of the cupboard, brought out the cherry brandy and three old-fashioned glasses engraved with vine-wreaths.

"It's a very cold night," she said, "and maybe you'd like a sip of this cordial. It was made a great while ago by our grandmother."

"It looks fine," said Mr. Ramy bowing, and Ann Eliza filled the glasses. In her own and Evelina's she poured only a few drops, but she filled their guest's to the brim. "My sister and I seldom take wine," she explained.

With another bow, which included both his hostesses, Mr. Ramy drank off the cherry brandy and pronounced it excellent.

Evelina meanwhile, with an assumption of industry intended to put their guest at ease, had taken up her instruments and was twisting a rose-petal into shape.

"You make artificial flowers, I see, ma'am," said Mr. Ramy with interest. "It's very pretty work. I had a lady-vriend in Shermany dat used to make flowers." He put out a square finger-tip to touch the petal.

Evelina blushed a little. "You left Germany long ago, I suppose?"

"Dear me yes, a goot while ago. I was only ninedeen when I come to the States."

After this the conversation dragged on intermittently till Mr. Ramy, peering about the room with the short-sighted glance of his race, said with an air of interest: "You're pleasantly fixed here; it looks real cosy." The note of wistfulness in his voice was obscurely moving to Ann Eliza.

"Oh, we live very plainly," said Evelina, with an affectation of grandeur deeply impressive to her sister. "We have very simple tastes."

"You look real comfortable, anyhow," said Mr. Ramy. His bulging eyes seemed to muster the details of the scene with a gentle envy. "I wisht I had as good a store; but I guess no blace seems home-like when you're always alone in it."

For some minutes longer the conversation moved on at this desultory pace, and then Mr. Ramy, who had been obviously nerving himself for the difficult act of departure, took his leave with an abruptness which would have startled anyone used to the subtler gradations of intercourse. But to Ann Eliza and her sister there was nothing surprising in his abrupt retreat. The long-drawn agonies of preparing to leave, and the subsequent dumb plunge through the door, were so usual in their circle that they would have been as much embarrassed as Mr. Ramy if he had tried to put any fluency into his adieux.

After he had left both sisters remained silent for a while; then Evelina, laying aside her unfinished flower, said: "I'll go and lock up."

IV

Intolerably monotonous seemed now to the Bunner sisters the treadmill routine of the shop, colourless and long their evenings about the lamp, aimless their habitual interchange of words to the weary accompaniment of the sewing and pinking machines.

It was perhaps with the idea of relieving the tension of their mood that Evelina, the following Sunday, suggested inviting Miss Mellins to supper. The Bunner sisters were not in a position to be lavish of the humblest hospitality, but two or three times in the year they shared their evening meal with a friend; and Miss Mellins, still flushed with the importance of her "turn," seemed the most interesting guest they could invite.

As the three women seated themselves at the supper-table, embellished by the unwonted addition of pound cake and sweet pickles, the dress-maker's sharp swarthy person stood out vividly between the neutral-tinted sisters. Miss Mellins was a small woman with a glossy yellow face and a frizz of black hair bristling with imitation tortoise-shell pins. Her sleeves had a fashionable cut, and half a dozen metal bangles rattled on her wrists. Her voice rattled like her bangles as she poured forth a stream of anecdote and ejaculation; and her round black eyes jumped with acrobatic velocity from one face to another. Miss Mellins was always having or hearing of amazing adventures. She had surprised a burglar in her room at midnight (though how he got there, what he robbed her of, and by what means he escaped had never been quite clear to her auditors); she had been warned by anonymous letters that her grocer (a rejected suitor) was putting poison in her tea; she had a customer who was shadowed by detectives, and another (a very wealthy lady) who had been arrested in a department store for kleptomania; she had been present at a spiritualist seance where an old gentleman had died in a fit on seeing a materialization of his mother-in-law; she had escaped from two fires in her night-gown, and at the funeral of her first cousin the horses attached to the hearse had run away and smashed the coffin, precipitating her relative into an open man-hole before the eyes of his distracted family.

A sceptical observer might have explained Miss Mellins's proneness to adventure by the fact that she derived her chief mental nourishment from the Police Gazette and the Fireside Weekly; but her lot was cast in a circle where such insinuations were not likely to be heard, and where the title-role in blood-curdling drama had long been her recognized right.

"Yes," she was now saying, her emphatic eyes on Ann Eliza, "you may not believe it, Miss Bunner, and I don't know's I should myself if anybody else was to tell me, but over a year before ever I was born, my mother she went to see a gypsy fortune-teller that was exhibited in a tent on the Battery with the green-headed lady, though her father warned her not to—and what you s'pose she told her? Why, she told her these very words—says she: 'Your next child'll be a girl with jet-black curls, and she'll suffer from spasms.'"

"Mercy!" murmured Ann Eliza, a ripple of sympathy running down her spine.

"D'you ever have spasms before, Miss Mellins?" Evelina asked.

"Yes, ma'am," the dress-maker declared. "And where'd you suppose I had 'em? Why, at my cousin Emma McIntyre's wedding, her that married the apothecary over in Jersey City, though her mother appeared to her in a dream and told her she'd rue the day she done it, but as Emma said, she got more advice than she wanted from the living, and if she was to listen to spectres too she'd never be sure what she'd ought to do and what she'd oughtn't; but I will say her husband took to drink, and she never was the same woman after her fust baby, well, they had an elegant church wedding, and what you s'pose I saw as I was walkin' up the aisle with the wedding percession?"

"Well?" Ann Eliza whispered, forgetting to thread her needle.

"Why, a coffin, to be sure, right on the top step of the chancel, Emma's folks is 'piscopalians and she would have a church wedding, though HIS mother raised a terrible rumpus over it, well, there it set, right in front of where the minister stood that was going to marry 'em, a coffin covered with a black velvet pall with a gold fringe, and a 'Gates Ajar' in white camellias atop of it."

"Goodness," said Evelina, starting, "there's a knock!"

"Who can it be?" shuddered Ann Eliza, still under the spell of Miss Mellins's hallucination.

Evelina rose and lit a candle to guide her through the shop. They heard her turn the key of the outer door, and a gust of night air stirred the close atmosphere of the back room; then there was a sound of vivacious exclamations, and Evelina returned with Mr. Ramy.

Ann Eliza's heart rocked like a boat in a heavy sea, and the dress-maker's eyes, distended with curiosity, sprang eagerly from face to face.

"I just thought I'd call in again," said Mr. Ramy, evidently somewhat disconcerted by the presence of Miss Mellins. "Just to see how the clock's behaving," he added with his hollow-cheeked smile.

"Oh, she's behaving beautiful," said Ann Eliza; "but we're real glad to see you all the same. Miss Mellins, let me make you acquainted with Mr. Ramy."

The dress-maker tossed back her head and dropped her lids in condescending recognition of the stranger's presence; and Mr. Ramy responded by an awkward bow. After the first moment of constraint a renewed sense of satisfaction filled the consciousness of the three women. The Bunner sisters were not sorry to let Miss Mellins see that they received an occasional evening visit, and Miss Mellins was clearly enchanted at the opportunity of pouring her latest tale into a new ear. As for Mr. Ramy, he adjusted himself to the situation with greater ease than might have been expected, and Evelina, who had been sorry that he should enter the room while the remains of supper still lingered on the table, blushed with pleasure at his good-humored offer to help her "clear away."

The table cleared, Ann Eliza suggested a game of cards; and it was after eleven o'clock when Mr. Ramy rose to take leave. His adieux were so much less abrupt than on the occasion of his first visit that Evelina was able to satisfy her sense of etiquette by escorting him, candle in hand, to the outer door; and as the two disappeared into the shop Miss Mellins playfully turned to Ann Eliza.

"Well, well, Miss Bunner," she murmured, jerking her chin in the direction of the retreating figures, "I'd no idea your sister was keeping company. On'y to think!"

Ann Eliza, roused from a state of dreamy beatitude, turned her timid eyes on the dress-maker.

"Oh, you're mistaken, Miss Mellins. We don't har'ly know Mr. Ramy."

Miss Mellins smiled incredulously. "You go 'long, Miss Bunner. I guess there'll be a wedding somewhere round here before spring, and I'll be real offended if I ain't asked to make the dress. I've always seen her in a gored satin with rooshings."

Ann Eliza made no answer. She had grown very pale, and her eyes lingered searchingly on Evelina as the younger sister re-entered the room. Evelina's cheeks were pink, and her blue eyes glittered; but it seemed to Ann Eliza that the coquettish tilt of her head regrettably emphasized the weakness of her receding chin. It was the first time that Ann Eliza had ever seen a flaw in her sister's beauty, and her involuntary criticism startled her like a secret disloyalty.

That night, after the light had been put out, the elder sister knelt longer than usual at her prayers. In the silence of the darkened room she was offering up certain dreams and aspirations whose brief blossoming had lent a transient freshness to her days. She wondered now how she could ever have supposed that Mr. Ramy's visits had another cause than the one Miss Mellins suggested. Had not the sight of Evelina first inspired him with a sudden solicitude for the welfare of the clock? And what charms but Evelina's could have induced him to repeat his visit? Grief held up its torch to the frail fabric of Ann Eliza's illusions, and with a firm heart she watched them shrivel into ashes; then, rising from her knees full of the chill joy of renunciation, she laid a kiss on the crimping pins of the sleeping Evelina and crept under the bedspread at her side.

V

During the months that followed, Mr. Ramy visited the sisters with increasing frequency. It became his habit to call on them every Sunday evening, and occasionally during the week he would find an excuse for dropping in unannounced as they were settling down to their work beside the lamp. Ann Eliza noticed that Evelina now took the precaution of putting on her crimson bow every evening before supper, and that she had refurbished with a bit of carefully washed lace the black silk which they still called new because it had been bought a year after Ann Eliza's.

Mr. Ramy, as he grew more intimate, became less conversational, and after the sisters had blushingly accorded him the privilege of a pipe he began to permit himself long stretches of meditative silence that were not without charm to his hostesses. There was something at once fortifying and pacific in the sense of that tranquil male presence in an atmosphere which had so long quivered with little feminine doubts and distresses; and the sisters fell into the habit of saying to each other, in moments of uncertainty: "We'll ask Mr. Ramy when he comes," and of accepting his verdict, whatever it might be, with a fatalistic readiness that relieved them of all responsibility.

When Mr. Ramy drew the pipe from his mouth and became, in his turn, confidential, the acuteness of their sympathy grew almost painful to the sisters. With passionate participation they listened to the story of his early struggles in Germany, and of the long illness which had been the cause of his recent misfortunes. The name of the Mrs. Hochmuller (an old comrade's widow) who had nursed him through his fever was greeted with reverential sighs and an inward pang of envy whenever it recurred in his biographical monologues, and once when the sisters were alone Evelina called a responsive flush to Ann Eliza's brow by saying suddenly, without the mention of any name: "I wonder what she's like?"

One day toward spring Mr. Ramy, who had by this time become as much a part of their lives as the letter-carrier or the milkman, ventured the suggestion that the ladies should accompany him to an exhibition of stereopticon views which was to take place at Chickering Hall on the following evening.

After their first breathless "Oh!" of pleasure there was a silence of mutual consultation, which Ann Eliza at last broke by saying: "You better go with Mr. Ramy, Evelina. I guess we don't both want to leave the store at night."

Evelina, with such protests as politeness demanded, acquiesced in this opinion, and spent the next day in trimming a white chip bonnet with forget-me-nots of her own making. Ann Eliza brought out her mosaic brooch, a cashmere scarf of their mother's was taken from its linen cerements, and thus adorned Evelina blushingly departed with Mr. Ramy, while the elder sister sat down in her place at the pinking-machine.

It seemed to Ann Eliza that she was alone for hours, and she was surprised, when she heard Evelina tap on the door, to find that the clock marked only half-past ten.

"It must have gone wrong again," she reflected as she rose to let her sister in.

The evening had been brilliantly interesting, and several striking stereopticon views of Berlin had afforded Mr. Ramy the opportunity of enlarging on the marvels of his native city.

"He said he'd love to show it all to me!" Evelina declared as Ann Eliza conned her glowing face. "Did you ever hear anything so silly? I didn't know which way to look."

Ann Eliza received this confidence with a sympathetic murmur.

"My bonnet IS becoming, isn't it?" Evelina went on irrelevantly, smiling at her reflection in the cracked glass above the chest of drawers.

"You're jest lovely," said Ann Eliza.

Spring was making itself unmistakably known to the distrustful New Yorker by an increased harshness of wind and prevalence of dust, when one day Evelina entered the back room at supper-time with a cluster of jonquils in her hand.

"I was just that foolish," she answered Ann Eliza's wondering glance, "I couldn't help buyin' 'em. I felt as if I must have something pretty to look at right away."

"Oh, sister," said Ann Eliza, in trembling sympathy. She felt that special indulgence must be conceded to those in Evelina's state since she had had her own fleeting vision of such mysterious longings as the words betrayed.

Evelina, meanwhile, had taken the bundle of dried grasses out of the broken china vase, and was putting the jonquils in their place with touches that lingered down their smooth stems and blade-like leaves.

"Ain't they pretty?" she kept repeating as she gathered the flowers into a starry circle. "Seems as if spring was really here, don't it?"

Ann Eliza remembered that it was Mr. Ramy's evening.

When he came, the Teutonic eye for anything that blooms made him turn at once to the jonquils.

"Ain't dey pretty?" he said. "Seems like as if de spring was really here."

"Don't it?" Evelina exclaimed, thrilled by the coincidence of their thought. "It's just what I was saying to my sister."

Ann Eliza got up suddenly and moved away; she remembered that she had not wound the clock the day before. Evelina was sitting at the table; the jonquils rose slenderly between herself and Mr. Ramy.

"Oh," she murmured with vague eyes, "how I'd love to get away somewheres into the country this very minute, somewheres where it was green and quiet. Seems as if I couldn't stand the city another day." But Ann Eliza noticed that she was looking at Mr. Ramy, and not at the flowers.

"I guess we might go to Cendral Park some Sunday," their visitor suggested. "Do you ever go there, Miss Evelina?"

"No, we don't very often; leastways we ain't been for a good while." She sparkled at the prospect. "It would be lovely, wouldn't it, Ann Eliza?"

"Why, yes," said the elder sister, coming back to her seat.

"Well, why don't we go next Sunday?" Mr. Ramy continued. "And we'll invite Miss Mellins too, that'll make a gosy little party."

That night when Evelina undressed she took a jonquil from the vase and pressed it with a certain ostentation between the leaves of her prayer-book. Ann Eliza, covertly observing her, felt that Evelina was not sorry to be observed, and that her own acute consciousness of the act was somehow regarded as magnifying its significance.

The following Sunday broke blue and warm. The Bunner sisters were habitual church-goers, but for once they left their prayer-books on the what-not, and ten o'clock found them, gloved and bonneted, awaiting Miss Mellins's knock. Miss Mellins presently appeared in a glitter of jet sequins and spangles, with a tale of having seen a strange man prowling under her windows till he was called off at dawn by a confederate's whistle; and shortly afterward came Mr. Ramy, his hair brushed with more than usual care, his broad hands encased in gloves of olive-green kid.

The little party set out for the nearest street-car, and a flutter of mingled gratification and embarrassment stirred Ann Eliza's bosom when it was found that Mr. Ramy intended to pay their fares. Nor did he fail to live up to this opening liberality; for after guiding them through the Mall and the Ramble he led the way to a rustic restaurant where, also at his expense, they fared idyllically on milk and lemon-pie.

After this they resumed their walk, strolling on with the slowness of unaccustomed holiday-makers from one path to another, through budding shrubberies, past grass-banks sprinkled with lilac crocuses, and under rocks on which the forsythia lay like sudden sunshine. Everything about her seemed new and miraculously lovely to Ann Eliza; but she kept her feelings to herself, leaving it to Evelina to exclaim at the hepaticas under the shady ledges, and to Miss Mellins, less interested in the vegetable than in the human world, to remark significantly on the probable history of the persons they met. All the alleys were thronged with promenaders and obstructed by perambulators; and Miss Mellins's running commentary threw a glare of lurid possibilities over the placid family groups and their romping progeny.

Ann Eliza was in no mood for such interpretations of life; but, knowing that Miss Mellins had been invited for the sole purpose of keeping her company she continued to cling to the dress-maker's side, letting Mr. Ramy lead the way with Evelina. Miss Mellins, stimulated by the excitement of the occasion, grew more and more discursive, and her ceaseless talk, and the kaleidoscopic whirl of the crowd, were unspeakably bewildering to Ann Eliza. Her feet, accustomed to the slippered ease of the shop, ached with the unfamiliar effort of walking, and her ears with the din of the dress-maker's anecdotes; but every nerve in her was aware of Evelina's enjoyment, and she was determined that no weariness of hers should curtail it. Yet even her heroism shrank from the significant glances which Miss Mellins presently began to cast at the couple in front of them: Ann Eliza could bear to connive at Evelina's bliss, but not to acknowledge it to others.

At length Evelina's feet also failed her, and she turned to suggest that they ought to be going home. Her flushed face had grown pale with fatigue, but her eyes were radiant.

The return lived in Ann Eliza's memory with the persistence of an evil dream. The horse-cars were packed with the returning throng, and they had to let a dozen go by before they could push their way into one that was already crowded. Ann Eliza had never before felt so tired. Even Miss Mellins's flow of narrative ran dry, and they sat silent, wedged between a negro woman and a pock-marked man with a bandaged head, while the car rumbled slowly down a squalid avenue to their corner. Evelina and Mr. Ramy sat together in the forward part of the car, and Ann Eliza could catch only an occasional glimpse of the forget-me-not bonnet and the clock-maker's shiny coat-collar; but when the little party got out at their corner the crowd swept them together again, and they walked back in the effortless silence of tired children to the Bunner sisters' basement. As Miss Mellins and Mr. Ramy turned to go their various ways Evelina mustered a last display of smiles; but Ann Eliza crossed the threshold in silence, feeling the stillness of the little shop reach out to her like consoling arms.

That night she could not sleep; but as she lay cold and rigid at her sister's side, she suddenly felt the pressure of Evelina's arms, and heard her whisper: "Oh, Ann Eliza, warn't it heavenly?"

VI

For four days after their Sunday in the Park the Bunner sisters had no news of Mr. Ramy. At first neither one betrayed her disappointment and anxiety to the other; but on the fifth morning Evelina, always the first to yield to her feelings, said, as she turned from her untasted tea: "I thought you'd oughter take that money out by now, Ann Eliza."

Ann Eliza understood and reddened. The winter had been a fairly prosperous one for the sisters, and their slowly accumulated savings had now reached the handsome sum of two hundred dollars; but the satisfaction they might have felt in this unwonted opulence had been clouded by a suggestion of Miss Mellins's that there were dark rumours concerning the savings bank in which their funds were deposited. They knew Miss Mellins was given to vain alarms; but her words, by the sheer force of repetition, had so shaken Ann Eliza's peace that after long hours of midnight counsel the sisters had decided to advise with Mr. Ramy; and on Ann Eliza, as the head of the house, this duty had devolved. Mr. Ramy, when consulted, had not only confirmed the dress-maker's report, but had offered to find some safe investment which should give the sisters a higher rate of interest than the suspected savings bank; and Ann Eliza knew that Evelina alluded to the suggested transfer.

"Why, yes, to be sure," she agreed. "Mr. Ramy said if he was us he wouldn't want to leave his money there any longer'n he could help."

"It was over a week ago he said it," Evelina reminded her.

"I know; but he told me to wait till he'd found out for sure about that other investment; and we ain't seen him since then."

Ann Eliza's words released their secret fear. "I wonder what's happened to him," Evelina said. "You don't suppose he could be sick?"

"I was wondering too," Ann Eliza rejoined; and the sisters looked down at their plates.

"I should think you'd oughter do something about that money pretty soon," Evelina began again.

"Well, I know I'd oughter. What would you do if you was me?"

"If I was YOU," said her sister, with perceptible emphasis and a rising blush, "I'd go right round and see if Mr. Ramy was sick. YOU could."

The words pierced Ann Eliza like a blade. "Yes, that's so," she said.

"It would only seem friendly, if he really IS sick. If I was you I'd go to-day," Evelina continued; and after dinner Ann Eliza went.

On the way she had to leave a parcel at the dyer's, and having performed that errand she turned toward Mr. Ramy's shop. Never before had she felt so old, so hopeless and humble. She knew she was bound on a love-errand of Evelina's, and the knowledge seemed to dry the last drop of young blood in her veins. It took from her, too, all her faded virginal shyness; and with a brisk composure she turned the handle of the clock-maker's door.

But as she entered her heart began to tremble, for she saw Mr. Ramy, his face hidden in his hands, sitting behind the counter in an attitude of strange dejection. At the click of the latch he looked up slowly, fixing a lustreless stare on Ann Eliza. For a moment she thought he did not know her.

"Oh, you're sick!" she exclaimed; and the sound of her voice seemed to recall his wandering senses.

"Why, if it ain't Miss Bunner!" he said, in a low thick tone; but he made no attempt to move, and she noticed that his face was the colour of yellow ashes.

"You ARE sick," she persisted, emboldened by his evident need of help. "Mr. Ramy, it was real unfriendly of you not to let us know."

He continued to look at her with dull eyes. "I ain't been sick," he said. "Leastways not very: only one of my old turns." He spoke in a slow laboured way, as if he had difficulty in getting his words together.

"Rheumatism?" she ventured, seeing how unwillingly he seemed to move.

"Well, somethin' like, maybe. I couldn't hardly put a name to it."

"If it WAS anything like rheumatism, my grandmother used to make a tea—" Ann Eliza began: she had forgotten, in the warmth of the moment, that she had only come as Evelina's messenger.

At the mention of tea an expression of uncontrollable repugnance passed over Mr. Ramy's face. "Oh, I guess I'm getting on all right. I've just got a headache to-day."

Ann Eliza's courage dropped at the note of refusal in his voice.

"I'm sorry," she said gently. "My sister and me'd have been glad to do anything we could for you."

"Thank you kindly," said Mr. Ramy wearily; then, as she turned to the door, he added with an effort: "Maybe I'll step round to-morrow."

"We'll be real glad," Ann Eliza repeated. Her eyes were fixed on a dusty bronze clock in the window. She was unaware of looking at it at the time, but long afterward she remembered that it represented a Newfoundland dog with his paw on an open book.

When she reached home there was a purchaser in the shop, turning over hooks and eyes under Evelina's absent-minded supervision. Ann Eliza passed hastily into the back room, but in an instant she heard her sister at her side.

"Quick! I told her I was goin' to look for some smaller hooks, how is he?" Evelina gasped.

"He ain't been very well," said Ann Eliza slowly, her eyes on Evelina's eager face; "but he says he'll be sure to be round to-morrow night."

"He will? Are you telling me the truth?"

"Why, Evelina Bunner!"

"Oh, I don't care!" cried the younger recklessly, rushing back into the shop.

Ann Eliza stood burning with the shame of Evelina's self-exposure. She was shocked that, even to her, Evelina should lay bare the nakedness of her emotion; and she tried to turn her thoughts from it as though its recollection made her a sharer in her sister's debasement.

The next evening, Mr. Ramy reappeared, still somewhat sallow and red-lidded, but otherwise his usual self. Ann Eliza consulted him about the investment he had recommended, and after it had been settled that he should attend to the matter for her he took up the illustrated volume of Longfellow, for, as the sisters had learned, his culture soared beyond the newspapers, and read aloud, with a fine confusion of consonants, the poem on "Maidenhood." Evelina lowered her lids while he read. It was a very beautiful evening, and Ann Eliza thought afterward how different life might have been with a companion who read poetry like Mr. Ramy.

VII

During the ensuing weeks Mr. Ramy, though his visits were as frequent as ever, did not seem to regain his usual spirits. He complained frequently of headache, but rejected Ann Eliza's tentatively proffered remedies, and seemed to shrink from any prolonged investigation of his symptoms. July had come, with a sudden ardour of heat, and one evening, as the three sat together by the open window in the back room, Evelina said: "I dunno what I wouldn't give, a night like this, for a breath of real country air."

"So would I," said Mr. Ramy, knocking the ashes from his pipe. "I'd like to be setting in an arbour dis very minute."

"Oh, wouldn't it be lovely?"

"I always think it's real cool here, we'd be heaps hotter up where Miss Mellins is," said Ann Eliza.

"Oh, I daresay, but we'd be heaps cooler somewhere else," her sister snapped: she was not infrequently exasperated by Ann Eliza's furtive attempts to mollify Providence.

A few days later Mr. Ramy appeared with a suggestion which enchanted Evelina. He had gone the day before to see his friend, Mrs. Hochmuller, who lived in the outskirts of Hoboken, and Mrs. Hochmuller had proposed that on the following Sunday he should bring the Bunner sisters to spend the day with her.

"She's got a real garden, you know," Mr. Ramy explained, "wid trees and a real summer-house to set in; and hens and chickens too. And it's an elegant sail over on de ferry-boat."

The proposal drew no response from Ann Eliza. She was still oppressed by the recollection of her interminable Sunday in the Park; but, obedient to Evelina's imperious glance, she finally faltered out an acceptance.

The Sunday was a very hot one, and once on the ferry-boat Ann Eliza revived at the touch of the salt breeze, and the spectacle of the crowded waters; but when they reached the other shore, and stepped out on the dirty wharf, she began to ache with anticipated weariness. They got into a street-car, and were jolted from one mean street to another, till at length Mr. Ramy pulled the conductor's sleeve and they got out again; then they stood in the blazing sun, near the door of a crowded beer-saloon, waiting for another car to come; and that carried them out to a thinly settled district, past vacant lots and narrow brick houses standing in unsupported solitude, till they finally reached an almost rural region of scattered cottages and low wooden buildings that looked like village "stores." Here the car finally stopped of its own accord, and they walked along a rutty road, past a stone-cutter's yard with a high fence tapestried with theatrical advertisements, to a little red house with green blinds and a garden paling. Really, Mr. Ramy had not deceived them. Clumps of dielytra and day-lilies bloomed behind the paling, and a crooked elm hung romantically over the gable of the house.

At the gate Mrs. Hochmuller, a broad woman in brick-brown merino, met them with nods and smiles, while her daughter Linda, a flaxen-haired girl with mottled red cheeks and a sidelong stare, hovered inquisitively behind her. Mrs. Hochmuller, leading the way into the house, conducted the Bunner sisters the way to her bedroom. Here they were invited to spread out on a mountainous white featherbed the cashmere mantles under which the solemnity of the occasion had compelled them to swelter, and when they had given their black silks the necessary twitch of readjustment, and Evelina had fluffed out her hair before a looking-glass framed in pink-shell work, their hostess led them to a stuffy parlour smelling of gingerbread. After another ceremonial pause, broken by polite enquiries and shy ejaculations, they were shown into the kitchen, where the table was already spread with strange-looking spice-cakes and stewed fruits, and where they presently found themselves seated between Mrs. Hochmuller and Mr. Ramy, while the staring Linda bumped back and forth from the stove with steaming dishes.

To Ann Eliza the dinner seemed endless, and the rich fare strangely unappetizing. She was abashed by the easy intimacy of her hostess's voice and eye. With Mr. Ramy Mrs. Hochmuller was almost flippantly familiar, and it was only when Ann Eliza pictured her generous form bent above his sick-bed that she could forgive her for tersely addressing him as "Ramy." During one of the pauses of the meal Mrs. Hochmuller laid her knife and fork against the edges of her plate, and, fixing her eyes on the clock-maker's face, said accusingly: "You hat one of dem turns again, Ramy."

"I dunno as I had," he returned evasively.

Evelina glanced from one to the other. "Mr. Ramy HAS been sick," she said at length, as though to show that she also was in a position to speak with authority. "He's complained very frequently of headaches."

"Ho!—I know him," said Mrs. Hochmuller with a laugh, her eyes still on the clock-maker. "Ain't you ashamed of yourself, Ramy?"

Mr. Ramy, who was looking at his plate, said suddenly one word which the sisters could not understand; it sounded to Ann Eliza like "Shwike."

Mrs. Hochmuller laughed again. "My, my," she said, "wouldn't you think he'd be ashamed to go and be sick and never dell me, me that nursed him troo dat awful fever?"

"Yes, I SHOULD," said Evelina, with a spirited glance at Ramy; but he was looking at the sausages that Linda had just put on the table.

When dinner was over Mrs. Hochmuller invited her guests to step out of the kitchen-door, and they found themselves in a green enclosure, half garden, half orchard. Grey hens followed by golden broods clucked under the twisted apple-boughs, a cat dozed on the edge of an old well, and from tree to tree ran the network of clothes-line that denoted Mrs. Hochmuller's calling. Beyond the apple trees stood a yellow summer-house festooned with scarlet runners; and below it, on the farther side of a rough fence, the land dipped down, holding a bit of woodland in its hollow. It was all strangely sweet and still on that hot Sunday afternoon, and as she moved across the grass under the apple-boughs Ann Eliza thought of quiet afternoons in church, and of the hymns her mother had sung to her when she was a baby.

Evelina was more restless. She wandered from the well to the summer-house and back, she tossed crumbs to the chickens and disturbed the cat with arch caresses; and at last she expressed a desire to go down into the wood.

"I guess you got to go round by the road, then," said Mrs. Hochmuller. "My Linda she goes troo a hole in de fence, but I guess you'd tear your dress if you was to dry."

"I'll help you," said Mr. Ramy; and guided by Linda the pair walked along the fence till they reached a narrow gap in its boards. Through this they disappeared, watched curiously in their descent by the grinning Linda, while Mrs. Hochmuller and Ann Eliza were left alone in the summer-house.

Mrs. Hochmuller looked at her guest with a confidential smile. "I guess dey'll be gone quite a while," she remarked, jerking her double chin toward the gap in the fence. "Folks like dat don't never remember about de dime." And she drew out her knitting.

Ann Eliza could think of nothing to say.

"Your sister she thinks a great lot of him, don't she?" her hostess continued.

Ann Eliza's cheeks grew hot. "Ain't you a teeny bit lonesome away out here sometimes?" she asked. "I should think you'd be scared nights, all alone with your daughter."

"Oh, no, I ain't," said Mrs. Hochmuller. "You see I take in washing, dat's my business, and it's a lot cheaper doing it out here dan in de city: where'd I get a drying-ground like dis in Hobucken? And den it's safer for Linda too; it geeps her outer de streets."

"Oh," said Ann Eliza, shrinking. She began to feel a distinct aversion for her hostess, and her eyes turned with involuntary annoyance to the square-backed form of Linda, still inquisitively suspended on the fence. It seemed to Ann Eliza that Evelina and her companion would never return from the wood; but they came at length, Mr. Ramy's brow pearled with perspiration, Evelina pink and conscious, a drooping bunch of ferns in her hand; and it was clear that, to her at least, the moments had been winged.

"D'you suppose they'll revive?" she asked, holding up the ferns; but Ann Eliza, rising at her approach, said stiffly: "We'd better be getting home, Evelina."

"Mercy me! Ain't you going to take your coffee first?" Mrs. Hochmuller protested; and Ann Eliza found to her dismay that another long gastronomic ceremony must intervene before politeness permitted them to leave. At length, however, they found themselves again on the ferry-boat. Water and sky were grey, with a dividing gleam of sunset that sent sleek opal waves in the boat's wake. The wind had a cool tarry breath, as though it had travelled over miles of shipping, and the hiss of the water about the paddles was as delicious as though it had been splashed into their tired faces.

Ann Eliza sat apart, looking away from the others. She had made up her mind that Mr. Ramy had proposed to Evelina in the wood, and she was silently preparing herself to receive her sister's confidence that evening.

But Evelina was apparently in no mood for confidences. When they reached home she put her faded ferns in water, and after supper, when she had laid aside her silk dress and the forget-me-not bonnet, she remained silently seated in her rocking-chair near the open window. It was long since Ann Eliza had seen her in so uncommunicative a mood.

The following Saturday Ann Eliza was sitting alone in the shop when the door opened and Mr. Ramy entered. He had never before called at that hour, and she wondered a little anxiously what had brought him.

"Has anything happened?" she asked, pushing aside the basketful of buttons she had been sorting.

"Not's I know of," said Mr. Ramy tranquilly. "But I always close up the store at two o'clock Saturdays at this season, so I thought I might as well call round and see you."

"I'm real glad, I'm sure," said Ann Eliza; "but Evelina's out."

"I know dat," Mr. Ramy answered. "I met her round de corner. She told me she got to go to dat new dyer's up in Forty-eighth Street. She won't be back for a couple of hours, har'ly, will she?"

Ann Eliza looked at him with rising bewilderment. "No, I guess not," she answered; her instinctive hospitality prompting her to add: "Won't you set down jest the same?"

Mr. Ramy sat down on the stool beside the counter, and Ann Eliza returned to her place behind it.

"I can't leave the store," she explained.

"Well, I guess we're very well here." Ann Eliza had become suddenly aware that Mr. Ramy was looking at her with unusual intentness. Involuntarily her hand strayed to the thin streaks of hair on her temples, and thence descended to straighten the brooch beneath her collar.

"You're looking very well to-day, Miss Bunner," said Mr. Ramy, following her gesture with a smile.

"Oh," said Ann Eliza nervously. "I'm always well in health," she added.

"I guess you're healthier than your sister, even if you are less sizeable."

"Oh, I don't know. Evelina's a mite nervous sometimes, but she ain't a bit sickly."

"She eats heartier than you do; but that don't mean nothing," said Mr. Ramy.

Ann Eliza was silent. She could not follow the trend of his thought, and she did not care to commit herself farther about Evelina before she had ascertained if Mr. Ramy considered nervousness interesting or the reverse.

But Mr. Ramy spared her all farther indecision.

"Well, Miss Bunner," he said, drawing his stool closer to the counter, "I guess I might as well tell you fust as last what I come here for to-day. I want to get married."

Ann Eliza, in many a prayerful midnight hour, had sought to strengthen herself for the hearing of this avowal, but now that it had come she felt pitifully frightened and unprepared. Mr. Ramy was leaning with both elbows on the counter, and she noticed that his nails were clean and that he had brushed his hat; yet even these signs had not prepared her!

At last she heard herself say, with a dry throat in which her heart was hammering: "Mercy me, Mr. Ramy!"

"I want to get married," he repeated. "I'm too lonesome. It ain't good for a man to live all alone, and eat noding but cold meat every day."

"No," said Ann Eliza softly.

"And the dust fairly beats me."

"Oh, the dust, I know!"

Mr. Ramy stretched one of his blunt-fingered hands toward her. "I wisht you'd take me."

Still Ann Eliza did not understand. She rose hesitatingly from her seat, pushing aside the basket of buttons which lay between them; then she perceived that Mr. Ramy was trying to take her hand, and as their fingers met a flood of joy swept over her. Never afterward, though every other word of their interview was stamped on her memory beyond all possible forgetting, could she recall what he said while their hands touched; she only knew that she seemed to be floating on a summer sea, and that all its waves were in her ears.

"Me, me?" she gasped.

"I guess so," said her suitor placidly. "You suit me right down to the ground, Miss Bunner. Dat's the truth."

A woman passing along the street paused to look at the shop-window, and Ann Eliza half hoped she would come in; but after a desultory inspection she went on.

"Maybe you don't fancy me?" Mr. Ramy suggested, discountenanced by Ann Eliza's silence.

A word of assent was on her tongue, but her lips refused it. She must find some other way of telling him.

"I don't say that."

"Well, I always kinder thought we was suited to one another," Mr. Ramy continued, eased of his momentary doubt. "I always liked de quiet style, no fuss and airs, and not afraid of work." He spoke as though dispassionately cataloguing her charms.

Ann Eliza felt that she must make an end. "But, Mr. Ramy, you don't understand. I've never thought of marrying."

Mr. Ramy looked at her in surprise. "Why not?"

"Well, I don't know, har'ly." She moistened her twitching lips. "The fact is, I ain't as active as I look. Maybe I couldn't stand the care. I ain't as spry as Evelina, nor as young," she added, with a last great effort.

"But you do most of de work here, anyways," said her suitor doubtfully.

"Oh, well, that's because Evelina's busy outside; and where there's only two women the work don't amount to much. Besides, I'm the oldest; I have to look after things," she hastened on, half pained that her simple ruse should so readily deceive him.

"Well, I guess you're active enough for me," he persisted. His calm determination began to frighten her; she trembled lest her own should be less staunch.

"No, no," she repeated, feeling the tears on her lashes. "I couldn't, Mr. Ramy, I couldn't marry. I'm so surprised. I always thought it was Evelina, always. And so did everybody else. She's so bright and pretty, it seemed so natural."

"Well, you was all mistaken," said Mr. Ramy obstinately.

"I'm so sorry."

He rose, pushing back his chair.

"You'd better think it over," he said, in the large tone of a man who feels he may safely wait.

"Oh, no, no. It ain't any sorter use, Mr. Ramy. I don't never mean to marry. I get tired so easily, I'd be afraid of the work. And I have such awful headaches." She paused, racking her brain for more convincing infirmities.

"Headaches, do you?" said Mr. Ramy, turning back.

"My, yes, awful ones, that I have to give right up to. Evelina has to do everything when I have one of them headaches. She has to bring me my tea in the mornings."

"Well, I'm sorry to hear it," said Mr. Ramy.

"Thank you kindly all the same," Ann Eliza murmured. "And please don't—don't—" She stopped suddenly, looking at him through her tears.

"Oh, that's all right," he answered. "Don't you fret, Miss Gunner. Folks have got to suit themselves." She thought his tone had grown more resigned since she had spoken of her headaches.

For some moments he stood looking at her with a hesitating eye, as though uncertain how to end their conversation; and at length she found courage to say (in the words of a novel she had once read): "I don't want this should make any difference between us."

"Oh, my, no," said Mr. Ramy, absently picking up his hat.

"You'll come in just the same?" she continued, nerving herself to the effort. "We'd miss you awfully if you didn't. Evelina, she—" She paused, torn between her desire to turn his thoughts to Evelina, and the dread of prematurely disclosing her sister's secret.

"Don't Miss Evelina have no headaches?" Mr. Ramy suddenly asked.

"My, no, never—well, not to speak of, anyway. She ain't had one for ages, and when Evelina IS sick she won't never give in to it," Ann Eliza declared, making some hurried adjustments with her conscience.

"I wouldn't have thought that," said Mr. Ramy.

"I guess you don't know us as well as you thought you did."

"Well, no, that's so; maybe I don't. I'll wish you good day, Miss Bunner"; and Mr. Ramy moved toward the door.

"Good day, Mr. Ramy," Ann Eliza answered.

She felt unutterably thankful to be alone. She knew the crucial moment of her life had passed, and she was glad that she had not fallen below her own ideals. It had been a wonderful experience; and in spite of the tears on her cheeks she was not sorry to have known it. Two facts, however, took the edge from its perfection: that it had happened in the shop, and that she had not had on her black silk.

She passed the next hour in a state of dreamy ecstasy. Something had entered into her life of which no subsequent empoverishment could rob it: she glowed with the same rich sense of possessorship that once, as a little girl, she had felt when her mother had given her a gold locket and she had sat up in bed in the dark to draw it from its hiding-place beneath her night-gown.

At length a dread of Evelina's return began to mingle with these musings. How could she meet her younger sister's eye without betraying what had happened? She felt as though a visible glory lay on her, and she was glad that dusk had fallen when Evelina entered. But her fears were superfluous. Evelina, always self-absorbed, had of late lost all interest in the simple happenings of the shop, and Ann Eliza, with mingled mortification and relief, perceived that she was in no danger of being cross-questioned as to the events of the afternoon. She was glad of this; yet there was a touch of humiliation in finding that the portentous secret in her bosom did not visibly shine forth. It struck her as dull, and even slightly absurd, of Evelina not to know at last that they were equals.

PART II

VIII

Mr. Ramy, after a decent interval, returned to the shop; and Ann Eliza, when they met, was unable to detect whether the emotions which seethed under her black alpaca found an echo in his bosom. Outwardly he made no sign. He lit his pipe as placidly as ever and seemed to relapse without effort into the unruffled intimacy of old. Yet to Ann Eliza's initiated eye a change became gradually perceptible. She saw that he was beginning to look at her sister as he had looked at her on that momentous afternoon: she even discerned a secret significance in the turn of his talk with Evelina. Once he asked her abruptly if she should like to travel, and Ann Eliza saw that the flush on Evelina's cheek was reflected from the same fire which had scorched her own.

So they drifted on through the sultry weeks of July. At that season the business of the little shop almost ceased, and one Saturday morning Mr. Ramy proposed that the sisters should lock up early and go with him for a sail down the bay in one of the Coney Island boats.

Ann Eliza saw the light in Evelina's eye and her resolve was instantly taken.

"I guess I won't go, thank you kindly; but I'm sure my sister will be happy to."

She was pained by the perfunctory phrase with which Evelina urged her to accompany them; and still more by Mr. Ramy's silence.

"No, I guess I won't go," she repeated, rather in answer to herself than to them. "It's dreadfully hot and I've got a kinder headache."

"Oh, well, I wouldn't then," said her sister hurriedly. "You'd better jest set here quietly and rest."

"Yes, I'll rest," Ann Eliza assented.

At two o'clock Mr. Ramy returned, and a moment later he and Evelina left the shop. Evelina had made herself another new bonnet for the occasion, a bonnet, Ann Eliza thought, almost too youthful in shape and colour. It was the first time it had ever occurred to her to criticize Evelina's taste, and she was frightened at the insidious change in her attitude toward her sister.

When Ann Eliza, in later days, looked back on that afternoon she felt that there had been something prophetic in the quality of its solitude; it seemed to distill the triple essence of loneliness in which all her after-life was to be lived. No purchasers came; not a hand fell on the door-latch; and the tick of the clock in the back room ironically emphasized the passing of the empty hours.

Evelina returned late and alone. Ann Eliza felt the coming crisis in the sound of her footstep, which wavered along as if not knowing on what it trod. The elder sister's affection had so passionately projected itself into her junior's fate that at such moments she seemed to be living two lives, her own and Evelina's; and her private longings shrank into silence at the sight of the other's hungry bliss. But it was evident that Evelina, never acutely alive to the emotional atmosphere about her, had no idea that her secret was suspected; and with an assumption of unconcern that would have made Ann Eliza smile if the pang had been less piercing, the younger sister prepared to confess herself.

"What are you so busy about?" she said impatiently, as Ann Eliza, beneath the gas-jet, fumbled for the matches. "Ain't you even got time to ask me if I'd had a pleasant day?"

Ann Eliza turned with a quiet smile. "I guess I don't have to. Seems to me it's pretty plain you have."

"Well, I don't know. I don't know HOW I feel—it's all so queer. I almost think I'd like to scream."

"I guess you're tired."

"No, I ain't. It's not that. But it all happened so suddenly, and the boat was so crowded I thought everybody'd hear what he was saying. Ann Eliza," she broke out, "why on earth don't you ask me what I'm talking about?"

Ann Eliza, with a last effort of heroism, feigned a fond incomprehension.

"What ARE you?"

"Why, I'm engaged to be married, so there! Now it's out! And it happened right on the boat; only to think of it! Of course I wasn't exactly surprised, I've known right along he was going to sooner or later, on'y somehow I didn't think of its happening to-day. I thought he'd never get up his courage."

He said he was so 'fraid I'd say no, that's what kep' him so long from asking me. Well, I ain't said yes YET, leastways I told him I'd have to think it over; but I guess he knows. Oh, Ann Eliza, I'm so happy!" She hid the blinding brightness of her face.

Ann Eliza, just then, would only let herself feel that she was glad. She drew down Evelina's hands and kissed her, and they held each other. When Evelina regained her voice she had a tale to tell which carried their vigil far into the night. Not a syllable, not a glance or gesture of Ramy's, was the elder sister spared; and with unconscious irony she found herself comparing the details of his proposal to her with those which Evelina was imparting with merciless prolixity.

The next few days were taken up with the embarrassed adjustment of their new relation to Mr. Ramy and to each other. Ann Eliza's ardour carried her to new heights of self-effacement, and she invented late duties in the shop in order to leave Evelina and her suitor longer alone in the back room. Later on, when she tried to remember the details of those first days, few came back to her: she knew only that she got up each morning with the sense of having to push the leaden hours up the same long steep of pain.

Mr. Ramy came daily now. Every evening he and his betrothed went out for a stroll around the Square, and when Evelina came in her cheeks were always pink. "He's kissed her under that tree at the corner, away from the lamp-post," Ann Eliza said to herself, with sudden insight into unconjectured things. On Sundays they usually went for the whole afternoon to the Central Park, and Ann Eliza, from her seat in the mortal hush of the back room, followed step by step their long slow beatific walk.

There had been, as yet, no allusion to their marriage, except that Evelina had once told her sister that Mr. Ramy wished them to invite Mrs. Hochmuller and Linda to the wedding. The mention of the laundress raised a half-forgotten fear in Ann Eliza, and she said in a tone of tentative appeal: "I guess if I was you I wouldn't want to be very great friends with Mrs. Hochmuller."

Evelina glanced at her compassionately. "I guess if you was me you'd want to do everything you could to please the man you loved. It's lucky," she added with glacial irony, "that I'm not too grand for Herman's friends."

"Oh," Ann Eliza protested, "that ain't what I mean, and you know it ain't. Only somehow the day we saw her I didn't think she seemed like the kinder person you'd want for a friend."

"I guess a married woman's the best judge of such matters," Evelina replied, as though she already walked in the light of her future state.

Ann Eliza, after that, kept her own counsel. She saw that Evelina wanted her sympathy as little as her admonitions, and that already she counted for nothing in her sister's scheme of life. To Ann Eliza's idolatrous acceptance of the cruelties of fate this exclusion seemed both natural and just; but it caused her the most lively pain. She could not divest her love for Evelina of its passionate motherliness; no breath of reason could lower it to the cool temperature of sisterly affection.

She was then passing, as she thought, through the novitiate of her pain; preparing, in a hundred experimental ways, for the solitude awaiting her when Evelina left. It was true that it would be a tempered loneliness. They would not be far apart. Evelina would "run in" daily from the clock-maker's; they would doubtless take supper with her on Sundays. But already Ann Eliza guessed with what growing perfunctoriness her sister would fulfill these obligations; she even foresaw the day when, to get news of Evelina, she should have to lock the shop at nightfall and go herself to Mr.

Ramy's door. But on that contingency she would not dwell. "They can come to me when they want to, they'll always find me here," she simply said to herself.

One evening Evelina came in flushed and agitated from her stroll around the Square. Ann Eliza saw at once that something had happened; but the new habit of reticence checked her question.

She had not long to wait. "Oh, Ann Eliza, on'y to think what he says—" (the pronoun stood exclusively for Mr. Ramy). "I declare I'm so upset I thought the people in the Square would notice me. Don't I look queer? He wants to get married right off, this very next week."

"Next week?"

"Yes. So's we can move out to St. Louis right away."

"Him and you—move out to St. Louis?"

"Well, I don't know as it would be natural for him to want to go out there without me," Evelina simpered. "But it's all so sudden I don't know what to think. He only got the letter this morning. DO I look queer, Ann Eliza?" Her eye was roving for the mirror.

"No, you don't," said Ann Eliza almost harshly.

"Well, it's a mercy," Evelina pursued with a tinge of disappointment. "It's a regular miracle I didn't faint right out there in the Square. Herman's so thoughtless, he just put the letter into my hand without a word. It's from a big firm out there, the Tiff'ny of St. Louis, he says it is, offering him a place in their clock-department. Seems they heart of him through a German friend of his that's settled out there. It's a splendid opening, and if he gives satisfaction they'll raise him at the end of the year."

She paused, flushed with the importance of the situation, which seemed to lift her once for all above the dull level of her former life.

"Then you'll have to go?" came at last from Ann Eliza.

Evelina stared. "You wouldn't have me interfere with his prospects, would you?"

"No—no. I on'y meant—has it got to be so soon?"

"Right away, I tell you—next week. Ain't it awful?" blushed the bride.

Well, this was what happened to mothers. They bore it, Ann Eliza mused; so why not she? Ah, but they had their own chance first; she had had no chance at all. And now this life which she had made her own was going from her forever; had gone, already, in the inner and deeper sense, and was soon to vanish in even its outward nearness, its surface-communion of voice and eye. At that moment even the thought of Evelina's happiness refused her its consolatory ray; or its light, if she saw it, was too remote to warm her. The thirst for a personal and inalienable tie, for pangs and problems of her own, was parching Ann Eliza's soul: it seemed to her that she could never again gather strength to look her loneliness in the face.

The trivial obligations of the moment came to her aid. Nursed in idleness her grief would have mastered her; but the needs of the shop and the back room, and the preparations for Evelina's marriage, kept the tyrant under.

Miss Mellins, true to her anticipations, had been called on to aid in the making of the wedding dress, and she and Ann Eliza were bending one evening over the breadths of pearl-grey cashmere which in spite of the dress-maker's prophetic vision of gored satin, had been judged most suitable, when Evelina came into the room alone.

Ann Eliza had already had occasion to notice that it was a bad sign when Mr. Ramy left his affianced at the door. It generally meant that Evelina had something disturbing to communicate, and Ann Eliza's first glance told her that this time the news was grave.

Miss Mellins, who sat with her back to the door and her head bent over her sewing, started as Evelina came around to the opposite side of the table.

"Mercy, Miss Evelina! I declare I thought you was a ghost, the way you crep' in. I had a customer once up in Forty-ninth Street, a lovely young woman with a thirty-six bust and a waist you could ha' put into her wedding ring, and her husband, he crep' up behind her that way jest for a joke, and frightened her into a fit, and when she come to she was a raving maniac, and had to be taken to Bloomingdale with two doctors and a nurse to hold her in the carriage, and a lovely baby on'y six weeks old, and there she is to this day, poor creature."

"I didn't mean to startle you," said Evelina.

She sat down on the nearest chair, and as the lamp-light fell on her face Ann Eliza saw that she had been crying.

"You do look dead-beat," Miss Mellins resumed, after a pause of soul-probing scrutiny. "I guess Mr. Ramy lugs you round that Square too often. You'll walk your legs off if you ain't careful. Men don't never consider, they're all alike. Why, I had a cousin once that was engaged to a book-agent—"

"Maybe we'd better put away the work for to-night, Miss Mellins," Ann Eliza interposed. "I guess what Evelina wants is a good night's rest."

"That's so," assented the dress-maker. "Have you got the back breadths run together, Miss Bunner? Here's the sleeves. I'll pin 'em together." She drew a cluster of pins from her mouth, in which she seemed to secrete them as squirrels stow away nuts. "There," she said, rolling up her work, "you go right away to bed, Miss Evelina, and we'll set up a little later to-morrow night. I guess you're a mite nervous, ain't you? I know when my turn comes I'll be scared to death."

With this arch forecast she withdrew, and Ann Eliza, returning to the back room, found Evelina still listlessly seated by the table. True to her new policy of silence, the elder sister set about folding up the bridal dress; but suddenly Evelina said in a harsh unnatural voice: "There ain't any use in going on with that."

The folds slipped from Ann Eliza's hands.

"Evelina Bunner, what you mean?"

"Jest what I say. It's put off."

"Put off, what's put off?"

"Our getting married. He can't take me to St. Louis. He ain't got money enough." She brought the words out in the monotonous tone of a child reciting a lesson.

Ann Eliza picked up another breadth of cashmere and began to smooth it out. "I don't understand," she said at length.

"Well, it's plain enough. The journey's fearfully expensive, and we've got to have something left to start with when we get out there. We've counted up, and he ain't got the money to do it—that's all."

"But I thought he was going right into a splendid place."

"So he is; but the salary's pretty low the first year, and board's very high in St. Louis. He's jest got another letter from his German friend, and he's been figuring it out, and he's afraid to chance it. He'll have to go alone."

"But there's your money, have you forgotten that? The hundred dollars in the bank."

Evelina made an impatient movement. "Of course I ain't forgotten it. On'y it ain't enough. It would all have to go into buying furniture, and if he was took sick and lost his place again we wouldn't have a cent left. He says he's got to lay by another hundred dollars before he'll be willing to take me out there."

For a while Ann Eliza pondered this surprising statement; then she ventured: "Seems to me he might have thought of it before."

In an instant Evelina was aflame. "I guess he knows what's right as well as you or me. I'd sooner die than be a burden to him."

Ann Eliza made no answer. The clutch of an unformulated doubt had checked the words on her lips. She had meant, on the day of her sister's marriage, to give Evelina the other half of their common savings; but something warned her not to say so now.

The sisters undressed without farther words. After they had gone to bed, and the light had been put out, the sound of Evelina's weeping came to Ann Eliza in the darkness, but she lay motionless on her own side of the bed, out of contact with her sister's shaken body. Never had she felt so coldly remote from Evelina.

The hours of the night moved slowly, ticked off with wearisome insistence by the clock which had played so prominent a part in their lives. Evelina's sobs still stirred the bed at gradually lengthening intervals, till at length Ann Eliza thought she slept. But with the dawn the eyes of the sisters met, and Ann Eliza's courage failed her as she looked in Evelina's face.

She sat up in bed and put out a pleading hand.

"Don't cry so, dearie. Don't."

"Oh, I can't bear it, I can't bear it," Evelina moaned.

Ann Eliza stroked her quivering shoulder. "Don't, don't," she repeated. "If you take the other hundred, won't that be enough? I always meant to give it to you. On'y I didn't want to tell you till your wedding day."

IX

Evelina's marriage took place on the appointed day. It was celebrated in the evening, in the chantry of the church which the sisters attended, and after it was over the few guests who had been present repaired to the Bunner Sisters' basement, where a wedding supper awaited them. Ann Eliza, aided by Miss Mellins and Mrs. Hawkins, and consciously supported by the sentimental interest of the whole street, had expended her utmost energy on the decoration of the shop and the back room. On the table a vase of white chrysanthemums stood between a dish of oranges and bananas and an iced wedding-cake wreathed with orange-blossoms of the bride's own making. Autumn leaves studded with paper roses festooned the what-not and the chromo of the Rock of Ages, and a wreath of yellow immortelles was twined about the clock which Evelina revered as the mysterious agent of her happiness.

At the table sat Miss Mellins, profusely spangled and bangled, her head sewing-girl, a pale young thing who had helped with Evelina's outfit, Mr. and Mrs. Hawkins, with Johnny, their eldest boy, and Mrs. Hochmuller and her daughter.

Mrs. Hochmuller's large blonde personality seemed to pervade the room to the effacement of the less amply-proportioned guests. It was rendered more impressive by a dress of crimson poplin that stood out from her in organ-like folds; and Linda, whom Ann Eliza had remembered as an uncouth child with a sly look about the eyes, surprised her by a sudden blossoming into feminine grace such as sometimes follows on a gawky girlhood. The Hochmullers, in fact, struck the dominant note in the entertainment. Beside them Evelina, unusually pale in her grey cashmere and white bonnet, looked like a faintly washed sketch beside a brilliant chromo; and Mr. Ramy, doomed to the traditional insignificance of the bridegroom's part, made no attempt to rise above his situation. Even Miss Mellins sparkled and jingled in vain in the shadow of Mrs. Hochmuller's crimson bulk; and Ann Eliza, with a sense of vague foreboding, saw that the wedding feast centred about the two guests she had most wished to exclude from it. What was said or done while they all sat about the table she never afterward recalled: the long hours remained in her memory as a whirl of high colours and loud voices, from which the pale presence of Evelina now and then emerged like a drowned face on a sunset-dabbled sea.

The next morning Mr. Ramy and his wife started for St. Louis, and Ann Eliza was left alone. Outwardly the first strain of parting was tempered by the arrival of Miss Mellins, Mrs. Hawkins and Johnny, who dropped in to help in the ungarlanding and tidying up of the back room. Ann Eliza was duly grateful for their kindness, but the "talking over" on which they had evidently counted was Dead Sea fruit on her lips; and just beyond the familiar warmth of their presences she saw the form of Solitude at her door.

Ann Eliza was but a small person to harbour so great a guest, and a trembling sense of insufficiency possessed her. She had no high musings to offer to the new companion of her hearth. Every one of her thoughts had hitherto turned to Evelina and shaped itself in homely easy words; of the mighty speech of silence she knew not the earliest syllable.

Everything in the back room and the shop, on the second day after Evelina's going, seemed to have grown coldly unfamiliar. The whole aspect of the place had changed with the changed conditions of Ann Eliza's life. The first customer who opened the shop-door startled her like a ghost; and all night she lay tossing on her side of the bed, sinking now and then into an uncertain doze from which she would suddenly wake to reach out her hand for Evelina. In the new silence surrounding her the walls and furniture found voice, frightening her at dusk and midnight with strange sighs and stealthy whispers. Ghostly hands shook the window shutters or rattled at the outer latch, and once she grew cold at the sound of a step like Evelina's stealing through the dark shop to die out on the threshold. In time, of course, she found an explanation for these noises, telling herself that the bedstead was warping, that Miss Mellins trod heavily overhead, or that the thunder of passing beer-waggons shook the door-latch; but the hours leading up to these conclusions were full of the floating terrors that harden into fixed foreboding. Worst of all were the solitary meals, when she absently continued to set aside the largest slice of pie for Evelina, and to let the tea grow cold while she waited for her sister to help herself to the first cup. Miss Mellins, coming in on one of these sad repasts, suggested the acquisition of a cat; but Ann Eliza shook her head. She had never been used to animals, and she felt the vague shrinking of the pious from creatures divided from her by the abyss of soullessness.

At length, after ten empty days, Evelina's first letter came.

"My dear Sister," she wrote, in her pinched Spencerian hand, "it seems strange to be in this great City so far from home alone with him I have chosen for life, but marriage has its solemn duties which those who are not can never hope to understand, and happier perhaps for this reason, life for them has only simple tasks and pleasures, but those who must take thought for others must be prepared to do their duty in whatever station it has pleased the Almighty to call them. Not that I have cause to complain, my dear Husband is all love and devotion, but being absent all day at his business how can I help but feel lonesome at times, as the poet says it is hard for they that love to live apart, and I often wonder, my dear Sister, how you are getting along alone in the store, may you never experience the feelings of solitude I have underwent since I came here. We are boarding now, but soon expect to find rooms and change our place of Residence, then I shall have all the care of a household to bear, but such is the fate of those who join their Lot with others, they cannot hope to escape from the burdens of Life, nor would I ask it, I would not live alway but while I live would always pray for strength to do my duty. This city is not near as large or handsome as New York, but had my lot been cast in a Wilderness I hope I should not repine, such never was my nature, and they who exchange their independence for the sweet name of Wife must be prepared to find all is not gold that glitters, nor I would not expect like you to drift down the stream of Life unfettered and serene as a Summer cloud, such is not my fate, but come what may will always find in me a resigned and prayerful Spirit, and hoping this finds you as well as it leaves me, I remain, my dear Sister,

"Yours truly,

"EVELINA B. RAMY."

Ann Eliza had always secretly admired the oratorical and impersonal tone of Evelina's letters; but the few she had previously read, having been addressed to school-mates or distant relatives, had appeared in the light of literary compositions rather than as records of personal experience. Now she could not but wish that Evelina had laid aside her swelling periods for a style more suited to the chronicling of homely incidents. She read the letter again and again, seeking for a clue to what her sister was really doing and thinking; but after each reading she emerged impressed but unenlightened from the labyrinth of Evelina's eloquence.

During the early winter she received two or three more letters of the same kind, each enclosing in its loose husk of rhetoric a smaller kernel of fact. By dint of patient interlinear study, Ann Eliza gathered from them that Evelina and her husband, after various costly experiments in boarding, had been reduced to a tenement-house flat; that living in St. Louis was more expensive than they had supposed, and that Mr. Ramy was kept out late at night (why, at a jeweller's, Ann Eliza wondered?) and found his position less satisfactory than he had been led to expect. Toward February the letters fell off; and finally they ceased to come.

At first Ann Eliza wrote, shyly but persistently, entreating for more frequent news; then, as one appeal after another was swallowed up in the mystery of Evelina's protracted silence, vague fears began to assail the elder sister. Perhaps Evelina was ill, and with no one to nurse her but a man who could not even make himself a cup of tea! Ann Eliza recalled the layer of dust in Mr. Ramy's shop, and pictures of domestic disorder mingled with the more poignant vision of her sister's illness. But surely if Evelina were ill Mr. Ramy would have written. He wrote a small neat hand, and epistolary communication was not an insuperable embarrassment to him. The too probable alternative was that both the unhappy pair had been prostrated by some disease which left them powerless to summon her, for summon her they surely would, Ann Eliza with unconscious cynicism reflected, if she or her small economies could be of use to them! The more she strained her eyes into the mystery, the darker it grew; and her lack of initiative, her inability to imagine what steps might be taken to trace the lost in distant places, left her benumbed and helpless.

At last there floated up from some depth of troubled memory the name of the firm of St. Louis jewellers by whom Mr. Ramy was employed. After much hesitation, and considerable effort, she addressed to them a timid request for news of her brother-in-law; and sooner than she could have hoped the answer reached her.

"DEAR MADAM,

"In reply to yours of the 29th ult. we beg to state the party you refer to was discharged from our employ a month ago. We are sorry we are unable to furnish you wish his address.

"Yours Respectfully,

"LUDWIG AND HAMMERBUSCH."

Ann Eliza read and re-read the curt statement in a stupor of distress. She had lost her last trace of Evelina. All that night she lay awake, revolving the stupendous project of going to St. Louis in search of her sister; but though she pieced together her few financial possibilities with the ingenuity of a brain used to fitting odd scraps into patch-work quilts, she woke to the cold daylight fact that she could not raise the money for her fare. Her wedding gift to Evelina had left her without any resources beyond her daily earnings, and these had steadily dwindled as the winter passed. She had long since renounced her weekly visit to the butcher, and had reduced her other expenses to the narrowest measure; but the most systematic frugality had not enabled her to put by any money. In spite of her dogged efforts to maintain the prosperity of the little shop, her sister's absence had already told on its business. Now that Ann Eliza had to carry the bundles to the dyer's herself, the customers who called in her absence, finding the shop locked, too often went elsewhere. Moreover, after several stern but unavailing efforts, she had had to give up the trimming of bonnets, which in Evelina's hands had been the most lucrative as well as the most interesting part of the business. This change, to the passing female eye, robbed the shop window of its chief attraction; and when painful experience had convinced the regular customers of the Bunner Sisters of Ann Eliza's lack of millinery skill they began to lose faith in her ability to curl a feather or even "freshen up" a bunch of flowers.

The time came when Ann Eliza had almost made up her mind to speak to the lady with puffed sleeves, who had always looked at her so kindly, and had once ordered a hat of Evelina. Perhaps the lady with puffed sleeves would be able to get her a little plain sewing to do; or she might recommend the shop to friends. Ann Eliza, with this possibility in view, rummaged out of a drawer the fly-blown remainder of the business cards which the sisters had ordered in the first flush of their commercial adventure; but when the lady with puffed sleeves finally appeared she was in deep mourning, and wore so sad a look that Ann Eliza dared not speak. She came in to buy some spools of black thread and silk, and in the doorway she turned back to say: "I am going away to-morrow for a long time. I hope you will have a pleasant winter." And the door shut on her.

One day not long after this it occurred to Ann Eliza to go to Hoboken in quest of Mrs. Hochmuller. Much as she shrank from pouring her distress into that particular ear, her anxiety had carried her beyond such reluctance; but when she began to think the matter over she was faced by a new difficulty. On the occasion of her only visit to Mrs. Hochmuller, she and Evelina had suffered themselves to be led there by Mr. Ramy; and Ann Eliza now perceived that she did not even know the name of the laundress's suburb, much less that of the street in which she lived. But she must have news of Evelina, and no obstacle was great enough to thwart her.

Though she longed to turn to some one for advice she disliked to expose her situation to Miss Mellins's searching eye, and at first she could think of no other confidant. Then she remembered Mrs. Hawkins, or rather her husband, who, though Ann Eliza had always thought him a dull uneducated man, was probably gifted with the mysterious masculine faculty of finding out people's addresses. It went hard with Ann Eliza to trust her secret even to the mild ear of Mrs. Hawkins, but at least she was spared the cross-examination to which the dress-maker would have subjected her. The accumulating pressure of domestic cares had so crushed in Mrs. Hawkins any curiosity concerning the affairs of others that she received her visitor's confidence with an almost masculine indifference, while she rocked her teething baby on one arm and with the other tried to check the acrobatic impulses of the next in age.

"My, my," she simply said as Ann Eliza ended. "Keep still now, Arthur: Miss Bunner don't want you to jump up and down on her foot to-day. And what are you gaping at, Johnny? Run right off and play," she added, turning sternly to her eldest, who, because he was the least naughty, usually bore the brunt of her wrath against the others.

"Well, perhaps Mr. Hawkins can help you," Mrs. Hawkins continued meditatively, while the children, after scattering at her bidding, returned to their previous pursuits like flies settling down on the spot from which an exasperated hand has swept them. "I'll send him right round the minute he comes in, and you can tell him the whole story. I wouldn't wonder but what he can find that Mrs. Hochmuller's address in the d'rectory. I know they've got one where he works."

"I'd be real thankful if he could," Ann Eliza murmured, rising from her seat with the factitious sense of lightness that comes from imparting a long-hidden dread.

X

Mr. Hawkins proved himself worthy of his wife's faith in his capacity. He learned from Ann Eliza as much as she could tell him about Mrs. Hochmuller and returned the next evening with a scrap of paper bearing her address, beneath which Johnny (the family scribe) had written in a large round hand the names of the streets that led there from the ferry.

Ann Eliza lay awake all that night, repeating over and over again the directions Mr. Hawkins had given her. He was a kind man, and she knew he would willingly have gone with her to Hoboken; indeed she read in his timid eye the half-formed intention of offering to accompany her, but on such an errand she preferred to go alone.

The next Sunday, accordingly, she set out early, and without much trouble found her way to the ferry. Nearly a year had passed since her previous visit to Mrs. Hochmuller, and a chilly April breeze smote her face as she stepped on the boat. Most of the passengers were huddled together in the cabin, and Ann Eliza shrank into its obscurest corner, shivering under the thin black mantle which had seemed so hot in July. She began to feel a little bewildered as she stepped ashore, but a paternal policeman put her into the right car, and as in a dream she found herself retracing the way to Mrs. Hochmuller's door. She had told the conductor the name of the street at which she wished to get out, and presently she stood in the biting wind at the corner near the beer-saloon, where the sun had once beat down on her so fiercely. At length an empty car appeared, its yellow flank emblazoned with the name of Mrs. Hochmuller's suburb, and Ann Eliza was presently jolting past the narrow brick houses islanded between vacant lots like giant piles in a desolate lagoon. When the car reached the end of its journey she got out and stood for some time trying to remember which turn Mr. Ramy had taken. She had just made up her mind to ask the car-driver when he shook the reins on the backs of his lean horses, and the car, still empty, jogged away toward Hoboken.

Ann Eliza, left alone by the roadside, began to move cautiously forward, looking about for a small red house with a gable overhung by an elm-tree; but everything about her seemed unfamiliar and forbidding. One or two surly looking men slouched past with inquisitive glances, and she could not make up her mind to stop and speak to them.

At length a tow-headed boy came out of a swinging door suggestive of illicit conviviality, and to him Ann Eliza ventured to confide her difficulty. The offer of five cents fired him with an instant willingness to lead her to Mrs. Hochmuller, and he was soon trotting past the stone-cutter's yard with Ann Eliza in his wake.

Another turn in the road brought them to the little red house, and having rewarded her guide Ann Eliza unlatched the gate and walked up to the door. Her heart was beating violently, and she had to lean against the door-post to compose her twitching lips: she had not known till that moment how much it was going to hurt her to speak of Evelina to Mrs. Hochmuller. As her agitation subsided she began to notice how much the appearance of the house had changed. It was not only that winter had stripped the elm, and blackened the flower-borders: the house itself had a debased and deserted air. The window-panes were cracked and dirty, and one or two shutters swung dismally on loosened hinges.

She rang several times before the door was opened. At length an Irish woman with a shawl over her head and a baby in her arms appeared on the threshold, and glancing past her into the narrow passage Ann Eliza saw that Mrs. Hochmuller's neat abode had deteriorated as much within as without.

At the mention of the name the woman stared. "Mrs. who, did ye say?"

"Mrs. Hochmuller. This is surely her house?"

"No, it ain't neither," said the woman turning away.

"Oh, but wait, please," Ann Eliza entreated. "I can't be mistaken. I mean the Mrs. Hochmuller who takes in washing. I came out to see her last June."

"Oh, the Dutch washerwoman is it, her that used to live here? She's been gone two months and more. It's Mike McNulty lives here now. Whisht!" to the baby, who had squared his mouth for a howl.

Ann Eliza's knees grew weak. "Mrs. Hochmuller gone? But where has she gone? She must be somewhere round here. Can't you tell me?"

"Sure an' I can't," said the woman. "She wint away before iver we come."

"Dalia Geoghegan, will ye bring the choild in out av the cowld?" cried an irate voice from within.

"Please wait, oh, please wait," Ann Eliza insisted. "You see I must find Mrs. Hochmuller."

"Why don't ye go and look for her thin?" the woman returned, slamming the door in her face.

She stood motionless on the door-step, dazed by the immensity of her disappointment, till a burst of loud voices inside the house drove her down the path and out of the gate.

Even then she could not grasp what had happened, and pausing in the road she looked back at the house, half hoping that Mrs. Hochmuller's once detested face might appear at one of the grimy windows.

She was roused by an icy wind that seemed to spring up suddenly from the desolate scene, piercing her thin dress like gauze; and turning away she began to retrace her steps. She thought of enquiring for Mrs. Hochmuller at some of the neighbouring houses, but their look was so unfriendly that she walked on without making up her mind at which door to ring. When she reached the horse-car terminus a car was just moving off toward Hoboken, and for nearly an hour she had to wait on the corner in the bitter wind. Her hands and feet were stiff with cold when the car at length loomed into sight again, and she thought of stopping somewhere on the way to the ferry for a cup of tea; but before the region of lunch-rooms was reached she had grown so sick and dizzy that the thought of food was repulsive. At length she found herself on the ferry-boat, in the soothing stuffiness of the crowded cabin; then came another interval of shivering on a street-corner, another long jolting journey in a "cross-town" car that smelt of damp straw and tobacco; and lastly, in the cold spring dusk, she unlocked her door and groped her way through the shop to her fireless bedroom.

The next morning Mrs. Hawkins, dropping in to hear the result of the trip, found Ann Eliza sitting behind the counter wrapped in an old shawl.

"Why, Miss Bunner, you're sick! You must have fever, your face is just as red!"

"It's nothing. I guess I caught cold yesterday on the ferry-boat," Ann Eliza acknowledged.

"And it's jest like a vault in here!" Mrs. Hawkins rebuked her. "Let me feel your hand—it's burning. Now, Miss Bunner, you've got to go right to bed this very minute."

"Oh, but I can't, Mrs. Hawkins." Ann Eliza attempted a wan smile. "You forget there ain't nobody but me to tend the store."

"I guess you won't tend it long neither, if you ain't careful," Mrs. Hawkins grimly rejoined. Beneath her placid exterior she cherished a morbid passion for disease and death, and the sight of Ann Eliza's suffering had roused her from her habitual indifference. "There ain't so many folks comes to the store anyhow," she went on with unconscious cruelty, "and I'll go right up and see if Miss Mellins can't spare one of her girls."

Ann Eliza, too weary to resist, allowed Mrs. Hawkins to put her to bed and make a cup of tea over the stove, while Miss Mellins, always good-naturedly responsive to any appeal for help, sent down the weak-eyed little girl to deal with hypothetical customers.

Ann Eliza, having so far abdicated her independence, sank into sudden apathy. As far as she could remember, it was the first time in her life that she had been taken care of instead of taking care, and there was a momentary relief in the surrender. She swallowed the tea like an obedient child, allowed a poultice to be applied to her aching chest and uttered no protest when a fire was kindled in the rarely used grate; but as Mrs. Hawkins bent over to "settle" her pillows she raised herself on her elbow to whisper: "Oh, Mrs. Hawkins, Mrs. Hochmuller warn't there." The tears rolled down her cheeks.

"She warn't there? Has she moved?"

"Over two months ago, and they don't know where she's gone. Oh what'll I do, Mrs. Hawkins?"

"There, there, Miss Bunner. You lay still and don't fret. I'll ask Mr. Hawkins soon as ever he comes home."

Ann Eliza murmured her gratitude, and Mrs. Hawkins, bending down, kissed her on the forehead. "Don't you fret," she repeated, in the voice with which she soothed her children.

For over a week Ann Eliza lay in bed, faithfully nursed by her two neighbours, while the weak-eyed child, and the pale sewing girl who had helped to finish Evelina's wedding dress, took turns in minding the shop. Every morning, when her friends appeared, Ann Eliza lifted her head to ask: "Is there a letter?" and at their gentle negative sank back in silence. Mrs. Hawkins, for several days, spoke no more of her promise to consult her husband as to the best way of tracing Mrs. Hochmuller; and dread of fresh disappointment kept Ann Eliza from bringing up the subject.

But the following Sunday evening, as she sat for the first time bolstered up in her rocking-chair near the stove, while Miss Mellins studied the Police Gazette beneath the lamp, there came a knock on the shop-door and Mr. Hawkins entered.

Ann Eliza's first glance at his plain friendly face showed her he had news to give, but though she no longer attempted to hide her anxiety from Miss Mellins, her lips trembled too much to let her speak.

"Good evening, Miss Bunner," said Mr. Hawkins in his dragging voice. "I've been over to Hoboken all day looking round for Mrs. Hochmuller."

"Oh, Mr. Hawkins—you HAVE?"

"I made a thorough search, but I'm sorry to say it was no use. She's left Hoboken, moved clear away, and nobody seems to know where."

"It was real good of you, Mr. Hawkins." Ann Eliza's voice struggled up in a faint whisper through the submerging tide of her disappointment.

Mr. Hawkins, in his embarrassed sense of being the bringer of bad news, stood before her uncertainly; then he turned to go. "No trouble at all," he paused to assure her from the doorway.

She wanted to speak again, to detain him, to ask him to advise her; but the words caught in her throat and she lay back silent.

The next day she got up early, and dressed and bonneted herself with twitching fingers. She waited till the weak-eyed child appeared, and having laid on her minute instructions as to the care of the shop, she slipped out into the street. It had occurred to her in one of the weary watches of the previous night that she might go to Tiffany's and make enquiries about Ramy's past. Possibly in that way she might obtain some information that would suggest a new way of reaching Evelina. She was guiltily aware that Mrs. Hawkins and Miss Mellins would be angry with her for venturing out of doors, but she knew she should never feel any better till she had news of Evelina.

The morning air was sharp, and as she turned to face the wind she felt so weak and unsteady that she wondered if she should ever get as far as Union Square; but by walking very slowly, and standing still now and then when she could do so without being noticed, she found herself at last before the jeweller's great glass doors.

It was still so early that there were no purchasers in the shop, and she felt herself the centre of innumerable unemployed eyes as she moved forward between long lines of show-cases glittering with diamonds and silver.

She was glancing about in the hope of finding the clock-department without having to approach one of the impressive gentlemen who paced the empty aisles, when she attracted the attention of one of the most impressive of the number.

The formidable benevolence with which he enquired what he could do for her made her almost despair of explaining herself; but she finally disentangled from a flurry of wrong beginnings the request to be shown to the clock-department.

The gentleman considered her thoughtfully. "May I ask what style of clock you are looking for? Would it be for a wedding-present, or—?"

The irony of the allusion filled Ann Eliza's veins with sudden strength. "I don't want to buy a clock at all. I want to see the head of the department."

"Mr. Loomis?" His stare still weighed her, then he seemed to brush aside the problem she presented as beneath his notice. "Oh, certainly. Take the elevator to the second floor. Next aisle to the left." He waved her down the endless perspective of show-cases.

Ann Eliza followed the line of his lordly gesture, and a swift ascent brought her to a great hall full of the buzzing and booming of thousands of clocks. Whichever way she looked, clocks stretched away from her in glittering interminable vistas: clocks of all sizes and voices, from the bell-throated giant of the hallway to the chirping dressing-table toy; tall clocks of mahogany and brass with cathedral chimes; clocks of bronze, glass, porcelain, of every possible size, voice and configuration; and between their serried ranks, along the polished floor of the aisles, moved the languid forms of other gentlemanly floor-walkers, waiting for their duties to begin.

One of them soon approached, and Ann Eliza repeated her request. He received it affably.

"Mr. Loomis? Go right down to the office at the other end." He pointed to a kind of box of ground glass and highly polished panelling.

As she thanked him he turned to one of his companions and said something in which she caught the name of Mr. Loomis, and which was received with an appreciative chuckle. She suspected herself of being the object of the pleasantry, and straightened her thin shoulders under her mantle.

The door of the office stood open, and within sat a gray-bearded man at a desk. He looked up kindly, and again she asked for Mr. Loomis.

"I'm Mr. Loomis. What can I do for you?"

He was much less portentous than the others, though she guessed him to be above them in authority; and encouraged by his tone she seated herself on the edge of the chair he waved her to.

"I hope you'll excuse my troubling you, sir. I came to ask if you could tell me anything about Mr. Herman Ramy. He was employed here in the clock-department two or three years ago."

Mr. Loomis showed no recognition of the name.

"Ramy? When was he discharged?"

"I don't har'ly know. He was very sick, and when he got well his place had been filled. He married my sister last October and they went to St. Louis, I ain't had any news of them for over two months, and she's my only sister, and I'm most crazy worrying about her."

"I see." Mr. Loomis reflected. "In what capacity was Ramy employed here?" he asked after a moment.

"He—he told us that he was one of the heads of the clock-department," Ann Eliza stammered, overswept by a sudden doubt.

"That was probably a slight exaggeration. But I can tell you about him by referring to our books. The name again?"

"Ramy, Herman Ramy."

There ensued a long silence, broken only by the flutter of leaves as Mr. Loomis turned over his ledgers. Presently he looked up, keeping his finger between the pages.

"Here it is, Herman Ramy. He was one of our ordinary workmen, and left us three years and a half ago last June."

"On account of sickness?" Ann Eliza faltered.

Mr. Loomis appeared to hesitate; then he said: "I see no mention of sickness." Ann Eliza felt his compassionate eyes on her again. "Perhaps I'd better tell you the truth. He was discharged for drug-taking. A capable workman, but we couldn't keep him straight. I'm sorry to have to tell you this, but it seems fairer, since you say you're anxious about your sister."

The polished sides of the office vanished from Ann Eliza's sight, and the cackle of the innumerable clocks came to her like the yell of waves in a storm. She tried to speak but could not; tried to get to her feet, but the floor was gone.

"I'm very sorry," Mr. Loomis repeated, closing the ledger. "I remember the man perfectly now. He used to disappear every now and then, and turn up again in a state that made him useless for days."

As she listened, Ann Eliza recalled the day when she had come on Mr. Ramy sitting in abject dejection behind his counter. She saw again the blurred unrecognizing eyes he had raised to her, the layer of dust over everything in the shop, and the green bronze clock in the window representing a Newfoundland dog with his paw on a book. She stood up slowly.

"Thank you. I'm sorry to have troubled you."

"It was no trouble. You say Ramy married your sister last October?"

"Yes, sir; and they went to St. Louis right afterward. I don't know how to find her. I thought maybe somebody here might know about him."

"Well, possibly some of the workmen might. Leave me your name and I'll send you word if I get on his track."

He handed her a pencil, and she wrote down her address; then she walked away blindly between the clocks.

XI

Mr. Loomis, true to his word, wrote a few days later that he had enquired in vain in the work-shop for any news of Ramy; and as she folded this letter and laid it between the leaves of her Bible, Ann Eliza felt that her last hope was gone. Miss Mellins, of course, had long since suggested the mediation of the police, and cited from her favourite literature convincing instances of the supernatural ability of the Pinkerton detective; but Mr. Hawkins, when called in council, dashed this project by remarking that detectives cost something like twenty dollars a day; and a vague fear of the law, some half-formed vision of Evelina in the clutch of a blue-coated "officer," kept Ann Eliza from invoking the aid of the police.

After the arrival of Mr. Loomis's note the weeks followed each other uneventfully. Ann Eliza's cough clung to her till late in the spring, the reflection in her looking-glass grew more bent and meagre, and her forehead sloped back farther toward the twist of hair that was fastened above her parting by a comb of black India-rubber.

Toward spring a lady who was expecting a baby took up her abode at the Mendoza Family Hotel, and through the friendly intervention of Miss Mellins the making of some of the baby-clothes was entrusted to Ann Eliza. This eased her of anxiety for the immediate future; but she had to rouse herself to feel any sense of relief. Her personal welfare was what least concerned her. Sometimes she thought of giving up the shop altogether; and only the fear that, if she changed her address, Evelina might not be able to find her, kept her from carrying out this plan.

Since she had lost her last hope of tracing her sister, all the activities of her lonely imagination had been concentrated on the possibility of Evelina's coming back to her. The discovery of Ramy's secret filled her with dreadful fears. In the solitude of the shop and the back room she was tortured by vague pictures of Evelina's sufferings. What horrors might not be hidden beneath her silence? Ann Eliza's great dread was that Miss Mellins should worm out of her what she had learned from Mr. Loomis. She was sure Miss Mellins must have abominable things to tell about drug-fiends—things she did not have the strength to hear. "Drug-fiend"—the very word was Satanic; she could hear Miss Mellins roll it on her tongue. But Ann Eliza's own imagination, left to itself, had begun to people the long hours with evil visions. Sometimes, in the night, she thought she heard herself called: the voice was her sister's, but faint with a nameless terror. Her most peaceful moments were those in which she managed to convince herself that Evelina was dead. She thought of her then, mournfully but more calmly, as thrust away under the neglected mound of some unknown cemetery, where no headstone marked her name, no mourner with flowers for another grave paused in pity to lay a blossom on hers. But this vision did not often give Ann Eliza its negative relief; and always, beneath its hazy lines, lurked the dark conviction that Evelina was alive, in misery and longing for her.

So the summer wore on. Ann Eliza was conscious that Mrs. Hawkins and Miss Mellins were watching her with affectionate anxiety, but the knowledge brought no comfort. She no longer cared what they felt or thought about her. Her grief lay far beyond touch of human healing, and after a while she became aware that they knew they could not help her. They still came in as often as their busy lives permitted, but their visits grew shorter, and Mrs. Hawkins always brought Arthur or the baby, so that there should be something to talk about, and some one whom she could scold.

The autumn came, and the winter. Business had fallen off again, and but few purchasers came to the little shop in the basement. In January Ann Eliza pawned her mother's cashmere scarf, her mosaic brooch, and the rosewood what-not on which the clock had always stood; she would have sold the bedstead too, but for the persistent vision of Evelina returning weak and weary, and not knowing where to lay her head.

The winter passed in its turn, and March reappeared with its galaxies of yellow jonquils at the windy street corners, reminding Ann Eliza of the spring day when Evelina had come home with a bunch of jonquils in her hand. In spite of the flowers which lent such a premature brightness to the streets the month was fierce and stormy, and Ann Eliza could get no warmth into her bones. Nevertheless, she was insensibly beginning to take up the healing routine of life. Little by little she had grown used to being alone, she had begun to take a languid interest in the one or two new purchasers the season had brought, and though the thought of Evelina was as poignant as ever, it was less persistently in the foreground of her mind.

Late one afternoon she was sitting behind the counter, wrapped in her shawl, and wondering how soon she might draw down the blinds and retreat into the comparative cosiness of the back room. She was not thinking of anything in particular, except perhaps in a hazy way of the lady with the puffed sleeves, who after her long eclipse had reappeared the day before in sleeves of a new cut, and bought some tape and needles. The lady still wore mourning, but she was evidently lightening it, and Ann Eliza saw in this the hope of future orders. The lady had left the shop about an hour before, walking away with her graceful step toward Fifth Avenue. She had wished Ann Eliza good day in her usual affable way, and Ann Eliza thought how odd it was that they should have been acquainted so long, and yet that she should not know the lady's name. From this consideration her mind wandered to the cut of the lady's new sleeves, and she was vexed with herself for not having noted it more carefully. She felt Miss Mellins might have liked to know about it. Ann Eliza's powers of observation had never been as keen as Evelina's, when the latter was not too self-absorbed to exert them. As Miss Mellins always said, Evelina could "take patterns with her eyes": she could have cut that new sleeve out of a folded newspaper in a trice! Musing on these things, Ann Eliza wished the lady would come back and give her another look at the sleeve. It was not unlikely that she might pass that way, for she certainly lived in or about the Square. Suddenly Ann Eliza remarked a small neat handkerchief on the counter: it must have dropped from the lady's purse, and she would probably come back to get it. Ann Eliza, pleased at the idea, sat on behind the counter and watched the darkening street. She always lit the gas as late as possible, keeping the box of matches at her elbow, so that if any one came she could apply a quick flame to the gas-jet. At length through the deepening dusk she distinguished a slim dark figure coming down the steps to the shop. With a little warmth of pleasure about her heart she reached up to light the gas. "I do believe I'll ask her name this time," she thought. She raised the flame to its full height, and saw her sister standing in the door.

There she was at last, the poor pale shade of Evelina, her thin face blanched of its faint pink, the stiff ripples gone from her hair, and a mantle shabbier than Ann Eliza's drawn about her narrow shoulders. The glare of the gas beat full on her as she stood and looked at Ann Eliza.

"Sister, oh, Evelina! I knowed you'd come!"

Ann Eliza had caught her close with a long moan of triumph. Vague words poured from her as she laid her cheek against Evelina's, trivial inarticulate endearments caught from Mrs. Hawkins's long discourses to her baby.

For a while Evelina let herself be passively held; then she drew back from her sister's clasp and looked about the shop. "I'm dead tired. Ain't there any fire?" she asked.

"Of course there is!" Ann Eliza, holding her hand fast, drew her into the back room. She did not want to ask any questions yet: she simply wanted to feel the emptiness of the room brimmed full again by the one presence that was warmth and light to her.

She knelt down before the grate, scraped some bits of coal and kindling from the bottom of the coal-scuttle, and drew one of the rocking-chairs up to the weak flame. "There—that'll blaze up in a minute," she said. She pressed Evelina down on the faded cushions of the rocking-chair, and, kneeling beside her, began to rub her hands.

"You're stone-cold, ain't you? Just sit still and warm yourself while I run and get the kettle. I've got something you always used to fancy for supper." She laid her hand on Evelina's shoulder. "Don't talk, oh, don't talk yet!" she implored. She wanted to keep that one frail second of happiness between herself and what she knew must come.

Evelina, without a word, bent over the fire, stretching her thin hands to the blaze and watching Ann Eliza fill the kettle and set the supper table. Her gaze had the dreamy fixity of a half-awakened child's.

Ann Eliza, with a smile of triumph, brought a slice of custard pie from the cupboard and put it by her sister's plate.

"You do like that, don't you? Miss Mellins sent it down to me this morning. She had her aunt from Brooklyn to dinner. Ain't it funny it just so happened?"

"I ain't hungry," said Evelina, rising to approach the table.

She sat down in her usual place, looked about her with the same wondering stare, and then, as of old, poured herself out the first cup of tea.

"Where's the what-not gone to?" she suddenly asked.

Ann Eliza set down the teapot and rose to get a spoon from the cupboard. With her back to the room she said: "The what-not? Why, you see, dearie, living here all alone by myself it only made one more thing to dust; so I sold it."

Evelina's eyes were still travelling about the familiar room. Though it was against all the traditions of the Bunner family to sell any household possession, she showed no surprise at her sister's answer.

"And the clock? The clock's gone too."

"Oh, I gave that away, I gave it to Mrs. Hawkins. She's kep' awake so nights with that last baby."

"I wish you'd never bought it," said Evelina harshly.

Ann Eliza's heart grew faint with fear. Without answering, she crossed over to her sister's seat and poured her out a second cup of tea. Then another thought struck her, and she went back to the cupboard and took out the cordial. In Evelina's absence considerable draughts had been drawn from it by invalid neighbours; but a glassful of the precious liquid still remained.

"Here, drink this right off, it'll warm you up quicker than anything," Ann Eliza said.

Evelina obeyed, and a slight spark of colour came into her cheeks. She turned to the custard pie and began to eat with a silent voracity distressing to watch. She did not even look to see what was left for Ann Eliza.

"I ain't hungry," she said at last as she laid down her fork. "I'm only so dead tired, that's the trouble."

"then you'd better get right into bed. Here's my old plaid dressing-gown, you remember it, don't you?" Ann Eliza laughed, recalling Evelina's ironies on the subject of the antiquated garment. With trembling fingers she began to undo her sister's cloak. The dress beneath it told a tale of poverty that Ann Eliza dared not pause to note. She drew it gently off, and as it slipped from Evelina's shoulders it revealed a tiny black bag hanging on a ribbon about her neck. Evelina lifted her hand as though to screen the bag from Ann Eliza; and the elder sister, seeing the gesture, continued her task with lowered eyes. She undressed Evelina as quickly as she could, and wrapping her in the plaid dressing-gown put her to bed, and spread her own shawl and her sister's cloak above the blanket.

"Where's the old red comfortable?" Evelina asked, as she sank down on the pillow.

"The comfortable? Oh, it was so hot and heavy I never used it after you went, so I sold that too. I never could sleep under much clothes."

She became aware that her sister was looking at her more attentively.

"I guess you've been in trouble too," Evelina said.

"Me? In trouble? What do you mean, Evelina?"

"You've had to pawn the things, I suppose," Evelina continued in a weary unmoved tone. "Well, I've been through worse than that. I've been to hell and back."

"Oh, Evelina, don't say it, sister!" Ann Eliza implored, shrinking from the unholy word. She knelt down and began to rub her sister's feet beneath the bedclothes.

"I've been to hell and back, if I AM back," Evelina repeated. She lifted her head from the pillow and began to talk with a sudden feverish volubility. "It began right away, less than a month after we were married. I've been in hell all that time, Ann Eliza." She fixed her eyes with passionate intentness on Ann Eliza's face. "He took opium. I didn't find it out till long afterward, at first, when he acted so strange, I thought he drank. But it was worse, much worse than drinking."

"Oh, sister, don't say it, don't say it yet! It's so sweet just to have you here with me again."

"I must say it," Evelina insisted, her flushed face burning with a kind of bitter cruelty. "You don't know what life's like, you don't know anything about it, setting here safe all the while in this peaceful place."

"Oh, Evelina, why didn't you write and send for me if it was like that?"

"That's why I couldn't write. Didn't you guess I was ashamed?"

"How could you be? Ashamed to write to Ann Eliza?"

Evelina raised herself on her thin elbow, while Ann Eliza, bending over, drew a corner of the shawl about her shoulder.

"Do lay down again. You'll catch your death."

"My death? That don't frighten me! You don't know what I've been through." And sitting upright in the old mahogany bed, with flushed cheeks and chattering teeth, and Ann Eliza's trembling arm clasping the shawl about her neck, Evelina poured out her story. It was a tale of misery and humiliation so remote from the elder sister's innocent experiences that much of it was hardly intelligible to her. Evelina's dreadful familiarity with it all, her fluency about things which Ann Eliza half-guessed and quickly shuddered back from, seemed even more alien and terrible than the actual tale she told. It was one thing, and heaven knew it was bad enough!—to learn that one's sister's husband was a drug-fiend; it was another, and much worse thing, to learn from that sister's pallid lips what vileness lay behind the word.

Evelina, unconscious of any distress but her own, sat upright, shivering in Ann Eliza's hold, while she piled up, detail by detail, her dreary narrative.

"The minute we got out there, and he found the job wasn't as good as he expected, he changed. At first I thought he was sick, I used to try to keep him home and nurse him. Then I saw it was something different. He used to go off for hours at a time, and when he came back his eyes kinder had a fog over them. Sometimes he didn't har'ly know me, and when he did he seemed to hate me. Once he hit me here." She touched her breast. "Do you remember, Ann Eliza, that time he didn't come to see us for a week, the time after we all went to Central Park together, and you and I thought he must be sick?"

Ann Eliza nodded.

"Well, that was the trouble, he'd been at it then. But nothing like as bad. After we'd been out there about a month he disappeared for a whole week. They took him back at the store, and gave him another chance; but the second time they discharged him, and he drifted round for ever so long before he could get another job. We spent all our money and had to move to a cheaper place. Then he got something to do, but they hardly paid him anything, and he didn't stay there long. When he found out about the baby—"

"The baby?" Ann Eliza faltered.

"It's dead, it only lived a day. When he found out about it, he got mad, and said he hadn't any money to pay doctors' bills, and I'd better write to you to help us. He had an idea you had money hidden away that I didn't know about." She turned to her sister with remorseful eyes. "It was him that made me get that hundred dollars out of you."

"Hush, hush. I always meant it for you anyhow."

"Yes, but I wouldn't have taken it if he hadn't been at me the whole time. He used to make me do just what he wanted. Well, when I said I wouldn't write to you for more money he said I'd better try and earn some myself. That was when he struck me. . . . Oh, you don't know what I'm talking about yet! . . . I tried to get work at a milliner's, but I was so sick I couldn't stay. I was sick all the time. I wisht I'd ha' died, Ann Eliza."

"No, no, Evelina."

"Yes, I do. It kept getting worse and worse. We pawned the furniture, and they turned us out because we couldn't pay the rent; and so then we went to board with Mrs. Hochmuller."

Ann Eliza pressed her closer to dissemble her own tremor. "Mrs. Hochmuller?"

"Didn't you know she was out there? She moved out a month after we did. She wasn't bad to me, and I think she tried to keep him straight, but Linda—"

"Linda—?"

"Well, when I kep' getting worse, and he was always off, for days at a time, the doctor had me sent to a hospital."

"A hospital? Sister—sister!"

"It was better than being with him; and the doctors were real kind to me. After the baby was born I was very sick and had to stay there a good while. And one day when I was laying there Mrs. Hochmuller came in as white as a sheet, and told me him and Linda had gone off together and taken all her money. That's the last I ever saw of him." She broke off with a laugh and began to cough again.

Ann Eliza tried to persuade her to lie down and sleep, but the rest of her story had to be told before she could be soothed into consent. After the news of Ramy's flight she had had brain fever, and had been sent to another hospital where she stayed a long time, how long she couldn't remember. Dates and days meant nothing to her in the shapeless ruin of her life. When she left the hospital she found that Mrs. Hochmuller had gone too. She was penniless, and had no one to turn to. A lady visitor at the hospital was kind, and found her a place where she did housework; but she was so weak they couldn't keep her. Then she got a job as waitress in a down-town lunch-room, but one day she fainted while she was handing a dish, and that evening when they paid her they told her she needn't come again.

"After that I begged in the streets"—(Ann Eliza's grasp again grew tight)—"and one afternoon last week, when the matinees was coming out, I met a man with a pleasant face, something like Mr. Hawkins, and he stopped and asked me what the trouble was. I told him if he'd give me five dollars I'd have money enough to buy a ticket back to New York, and he took a good look at me and said, well, if that was what I wanted he'd go straight to the station with me and give me the five dollars there. So he did, and he bought the ticket, and put me in the cars."

Evelina sank back, her face a sallow wedge in the white cleft of the pillow. Ann Eliza leaned over her, and for a long time they held each other without speaking.

They were still clasped in this dumb embrace when there was a step in the shop and Ann Eliza, starting up, saw Miss Mellins in the doorway.

"My sakes, Miss Bunner! What in the land are you doing? Miss Evelina, Mrs. Ramy, it ain't you?"

Miss Mellins's eyes, bursting from their sockets, sprang from Evelina's pallid face to the disordered supper table and the heap of worn clothes on the floor; then they turned back to Ann Eliza, who had placed herself on the defensive between her sister and the dress-maker.

"My sister Evelina has come back, come back on a visit. she was taken sick in the cars on the way home, I guess she caught cold, so I made her go right to bed as soon as ever she got here."

Ann Eliza was surprised at the strength and steadiness of her voice. Fortified by its sound she went on, her eyes on Miss Mellins's baffled countenance: "Mr. Ramy has gone west on a trip, a trip connected with his business; and Evelina is going to stay with me till he comes back."

XII

What measure of belief her explanation of Evelina's return obtained in the small circle of her friends Ann Eliza did not pause to enquire. Though she could not remember ever having told a lie before, she adhered with rigid tenacity to the consequences of her first lapse from truth, and fortified her original statement with additional details whenever a questioner sought to take her unawares.

But other and more serious burdens lay on her startled conscience. For the first time in her life she dimly faced the awful problem of the inutility of self-sacrifice. Hitherto she had never thought of questioning the inherited principles which had guided her life. Self-effacement for the good of others had always seemed to her both natural and necessary; but then she had taken it for granted that it implied the securing of that good. Now she perceived that to refuse the gifts of life does not ensure their transmission to those for whom they have been surrendered; and her familiar heaven was unpeopled. She felt she could no longer trust in the goodness of God, and there was only a black abyss above the roof of Bunner Sisters.

But there was little time to brood upon such problems. The care of Evelina filled Ann Eliza's days and nights. The hastily summoned doctor had pronounced her to be suffering from pneumonia, and under his care the first stress of the disease was relieved. But her recovery was only partial, and long after the doctor's visits had ceased she continued to lie in bed, too weak to move, and seemingly indifferent to everything about her.

At length one evening, about six weeks after her return, she said to her sister: "I don't feel's if I'd ever get up again."

Ann Eliza turned from the kettle she was placing on the stove. She was startled by the echo the words woke in her own breast.

"Don't you talk like that, Evelina! I guess you're on'y tired out, and disheartened."

"Yes, I'm disheartened," Evelina murmured.

A few months earlier Ann Eliza would have met the confession with a word of pious admonition; now she accepted it in silence.

"Maybe you'll brighten up when your cough gets better," she suggested.

"Yes, or my cough'll get better when I brighten up," Evelina retorted with a touch of her old tartness.

"Does your cough keep on hurting you jest as much?"

"I don't see's there's much difference."

"Well, I guess I'll get the doctor to come round again," Ann Eliza said, trying for the matter-of-course tone in which one might speak of sending for the plumber or the gas-fitter.

"It ain't any use sending for the doctor, and who's going to pay him?"

"I am," answered the elder sister. "Here's your tea, and a mite of toast. Don't that tempt you?"

Already, in the watches of the night, Ann Eliza had been tormented by that same question, who was to pay the doctor?—and a few days before she had temporarily silenced it by borrowing twenty dollars of Miss Mellins. The transaction had cost her one of the bitterest struggles of her life. She had never borrowed a penny of any one before, and the possibility of having to do so had always been classed in her mind among those shameful extremities to which Providence does not let decent people come. But nowadays she no longer believed in the personal supervision of Providence; and had she been compelled to steal the money instead of borrowing it, she would have felt that her conscience was the only tribunal before which she had to answer. Nevertheless, the actual humiliation of having to ask for the money was no less bitter; and she could hardly hope that Miss Mellins would view the case with the same detachment as herself. Miss Mellins was very kind; but she not unnaturally felt that her kindness should be rewarded by according her the right to ask questions; and bit by bit Ann Eliza saw Evelina's miserable secret slipping into the dress-maker's possession.

When the doctor came she left him alone with Evelina, busying herself in the shop that she might have an opportunity of seeing him alone on his way out. To steady herself she began to sort a trayful of buttons, and when the doctor appeared she was reciting under her breath: "Twenty-four horn, two and a half cards fancy pearl . . ." She saw at once that his look was grave.

He sat down on the chair beside the counter, and her mind travelled miles before he spoke.

"Miss Bunner, the best thing you can do is to let me get a bed for your sister at St. Luke's."

"The hospital?"

"Come now, you're above that sort of prejudice, aren't you?" The doctor spoke in the tone of one who coaxes a spoiled child. "I know how devoted you are, but Mrs. Ramy can be much better cared for there than here. You really haven't time to look after her and attend to your business as well. There'll be no expense, you understand—"

Ann Eliza made no answer. "You think my sister's going to be sick a good while, then?" she asked.

"Well, yes, possibly."

"You think she's very sick?"

"Well, yes. She's very sick."

His face had grown still graver; he sat there as though he had never known what it was to hurry.

Ann Eliza continued to separate the pearl and horn buttons. Suddenly she lifted her eyes and looked at him. "Is she going to die?"

The doctor laid a kindly hand on hers. "We never say that, Miss Bunner. Human skill works wonders, and at the hospital Mrs. Ramy would have every chance."

"What is it? What's she dying of?"

The doctor hesitated, seeking to substitute a popular phrase for the scientific terminology which rose to his lips.

"I want to know," Ann Eliza persisted.

"Yes, of course; I understand. Well, your sister has had a hard time lately, and there is a complication of causes, resulting in consumption, rapid consumption. At the hospital—"

"I'll keep her here," said Ann Eliza quietly.

After the doctor had gone she went on for some time sorting the buttons; then she slipped the tray into its place on a shelf behind the counter and went into the back room. She found Evelina propped upright against the pillows, a flush of agitation on her cheeks. Ann Eliza pulled up the shawl which had slipped from her sister's shoulders.

"How long you've been! What's he been saying?"

"Oh, he went long ago, he on'y stopped to give me a prescription. I was sorting out that tray of buttons. Miss Mellins's girl got them all mixed up."

She felt Evelina's eyes upon her.

"He must have said something: what was it?"

"Why, he said you'd have to be careful, and stay in bed, and take this new medicine he's given you."

"Did he say I was going to get well?"

"Why, Evelina!"

"What's the use, Ann Eliza? You can't deceive me. I've just been up to look at myself in the glass; and I saw plenty of 'em in the hospital that looked like me. They didn't get well, and I ain't going to." Her head dropped back. "It don't much matter—I'm about tired. On'y there's one thing—Ann Eliza—"

The elder sister drew near to the bed.

"There's one thing I ain't told you. I didn't want to tell you yet because I was afraid you might be sorry, but if he says I'm going to die I've got to say it." She stopped to cough, and to Ann Eliza it now seemed as though every cough struck a minute from the hours remaining to her.

"Don't talk now, you're tired."

"I'll be tireder to-morrow, I guess. And I want you should know. Sit down close to me—there."

Ann Eliza sat down in silence, stroking her shrunken hand.

"I'm a Roman Catholic, Ann Eliza."

"Evelina, oh, Evelina Bunner! A Roman Catholic—YOU? Oh, Evelina, did HE make you?"

Evelina shook her head. "I guess he didn't have no religion; he never spoke of it. But you see Mrs. Hochmuller was a Catholic, and so when I was sick she got the doctor to send me to a Roman Catholic hospital, and the sisters was so good to me there, and the priest used to come and talk to me; and the things he said kep' me from going crazy. He seemed to make everything easier."

"Oh, sister, how could you?" Ann Eliza wailed. She knew little of the Catholic religion except that "Papists" believed in it, in itself a sufficient indictment. Her spiritual rebellion had not freed her from the formal part of her religious belief, and apostasy had always seemed to her one of the sins from which the pure in mind avert their thoughts.

"And then when the baby was born," Evelina continued, "he christened it right away, so it could go to heaven; and after that, you see, I had to be a Catholic."

"I don't see—"

"Don't I have to be where the baby is? I couldn't ever ha' gone there if I hadn't been made a Catholic. Don't you understand that?"

Ann Eliza sat speechless, drawing her hand away. Once more she found herself shut out of Evelina's heart, an exile from her closest affections.

"I've got to go where the baby is," Evelina feverishly insisted.

Ann Eliza could think of nothing to say; she could only feel that Evelina was dying, and dying as a stranger in her arms. Ramy and the day-old baby had parted her forever from her sister.

Evelina began again. "If I get worse I want you to send for a priest. Miss Mellins'll know where to send, she's got an aunt that's a Catholic. Promise me faithful you will."

"I promise," said Ann Eliza.

After that they spoke no more of the matter; but Ann Eliza now understood that the little black bag about her sister's neck, which she had innocently taken for a memento of Ramy, was some kind of sacrilegious amulet, and her fingers shrank from its contact when she bathed and dressed Evelina. It seemed to her the diabolical instrument of their estrangement.

XIII

Spring had really come at last. There were leaves on the ailanthus-tree that Evelina could see from her bed, gentle clouds floated over it in the blue, and now and then the cry of a flower-seller sounded from the street.

One day there was a shy knock on the back-room door, and Johnny Hawkins came in with two yellow jonquils in his fist. He was getting bigger and squarer, and his round freckled face was growing into a smaller copy of his father's. He walked up to Evelina and held out the flowers.

"They blew off the cart and the fellow said I could keep 'em. But you can have 'em," he announced.

Ann Eliza rose from her seat at the sewing-machine and tried to take the flowers from him.

"They ain't for you; they're for her," he sturdily objected; and Evelina held out her hand for the jonquils.

After Johnny had gone she lay and looked at them without speaking. Ann Eliza, who had gone back to the machine, bent her head over the seam she was stitching; the click, click, click of the machine sounded in her ear like the tick of Ramy's clock, and it seemed to her that life had gone backward, and that Evelina, radiant and foolish, had just come into the room with the yellow flowers in her hand.

When at last she ventured to look up, she saw that her sister's head had drooped against the pillow, and that she was sleeping quietly. Her relaxed hand still held the jonquils, but it was evident that they had awakened no memories; she had dozed off almost as soon as Johnny had given them to her. The discovery gave Ann Eliza a startled sense of the ruins that must be piled upon her past. "I don't believe I could have forgotten that day, though," she said to herself. But she was glad that Evelina had forgotten.

Evelina's disease moved on along the usual course, now lifting her on a brief wave of elation, now sinking her to new depths of weakness. There was little to be done, and the doctor came only at lengthening intervals. On his way out he always repeated his first friendly suggestion about sending Evelina to the hospital; and Ann Eliza always answered: "I guess we can manage."

The hours passed for her with the fierce rapidity that great joy or anguish lends them. She went through the days with a sternly smiling precision, but she hardly knew what was happening, and when night-fall released her from the shop, and she could carry her work to Evelina's bedside, the same sense of unreality accompanied her, and she still seemed to be accomplishing a task whose object had escaped her memory.

Once, when Evelina felt better, she expressed a desire to make some artificial flowers, and Ann Eliza, deluded by this awakening interest, got out the faded bundles of stems and petals and the little tools and spools of wire. But after a few minutes the work dropped from Evelina's hands and she said: "I'll wait until to-morrow."

She never again spoke of the flower-making, but one day, after watching Ann Eliza's laboured attempt to trim a spring hat for Mrs. Hawkins, she demanded impatiently that the hat should be brought to her, and in a trice had galvanized the lifeless bow and given the brim the twist it needed.

These were rare gleams; and more frequent were the days of speechless lassitude, when she lay for hours silently staring at the window, shaken only by the hard incessant cough that sounded to Ann Eliza like the hammering of nails into a coffin.

At length one morning Ann Eliza, starting up from the mattress at the foot of the bed, hastily called Miss Mellins down, and ran through the smoky dawn for the doctor. He came back with her and did what he could to give Evelina momentary relief; then he went away, promising to look in again before night. Miss Mellins, her head still covered with curl-papers, disappeared in his wake, and when the sisters were alone Evelina beckoned to Ann Eliza.

"You promised," she whispered, grasping her sister's arm; and Ann Eliza understood. She had not yet dared to tell Miss Mellins of Evelina's change of faith; it had seemed even more difficult than borrowing the money; but now it had to be done. She ran upstairs after the dress-maker and detained her on the landing.

"Miss Mellins, can you tell me where to send for a priest, a Roman Catholic priest?"

"A priest, Miss Bunner?"

"Yes. My sister became a Roman Catholic while she was away. They were kind to her in her sickness, and now she wants a priest." Ann Eliza faced Miss Mellins with unflinching eyes.

"My aunt Dugan'll know. I'll run right round to her the minute I get my papers off," the dress-maker promised; and Ann Eliza thanked her.

An hour or two later the priest appeared. Ann Eliza, who was watching, saw him coming down the steps to the shop-door and went to meet him. His expression was kind, but she shrank from his peculiar dress, and from his pale face with its bluish chin and enigmatic smile. Ann Eliza remained in the shop. Miss Mellins's girl had mixed the buttons again and she set herself to sort them. The priest stayed a long time with Evelina. When he again carried his enigmatic smile past the counter, and Ann Eliza rejoined her sister, Evelina was smiling with something of the same mystery; but she did not tell her secret.

After that it seemed to Ann Eliza that the shop and the back room no longer belonged to her. It was as though she were there on sufferance, indulgently tolerated by the unseen power which hovered over Evelina even in the absence of its minister. The priest came almost daily; and at last a day arrived when he was called to administer some rite of which Ann Eliza but dimly grasped the sacramental meaning. All she knew was that it meant that Evelina was going, and going, under this alien guidance, even farther from her than to the dark places of death.

When the priest came, with something covered in his hands, she crept into the shop, closing the door of the back room to leave him alone with Evelina.

It was a warm afternoon in May, and the crooked ailanthus-tree rooted in a fissure of the opposite pavement was a fountain of tender green. Women in light dresses passed with the languid step of spring; and presently there came a man with a hand-cart full of pansy and geranium plants who stopped outside the window, signalling to Ann Eliza to buy.

An hour went by before the door of the back room opened and the priest reappeared with that mysterious covered something in his hands. Ann Eliza had risen, drawing back as he passed. He had doubtless divined her antipathy, for he had hitherto only bowed in going in and out; but to day he paused and looked at her compassionately.

"I have left your sister in a very beautiful state of mind," he said in a low voice like a woman's. "She is full of spiritual consolation."

Ann Eliza was silent, and he bowed and went out. She hastened back to Evelina's bed, and knelt down beside it. Evelina's eyes were very large and bright; she turned them on Ann Eliza with a look of inner illumination.

"I shall see the baby," she said; then her eyelids fell and she dozed.

The doctor came again at nightfall, administering some last palliatives; and after he had gone Ann Eliza, refusing to have her vigil shared by Miss Mellins or Mrs. Hawkins, sat down to keep watch alone.

It was a very quiet night. Evelina never spoke or opened her eyes, but in the still hour before dawn Ann Eliza saw that the restless hand outside the bed-clothes had stopped its twitching. She stooped over and felt no breath on her sister's lips.

The funeral took place three days later. Evelina was buried in Calvary Cemetery, the priest assuming the whole care of the necessary arrangements, while Ann Eliza, a passive spectator, beheld with stony indifference this last negation of her past.

A week afterward she stood in her bonnet and mantle in the doorway of the little shop. Its whole aspect had changed. Counter and shelves were bare, the window was stripped of its familiar miscellany of artificial flowers, note-paper, wire hat-frames, and limp garments from the dyer's; and against the glass pane of the doorway hung a sign: "This store to let."

Ann Eliza turned her eyes from the sign as she went out and locked the door behind her. Evelina's funeral had been very expensive, and Ann Eliza, having sold her stock-in-trade and the few articles of furniture that remained to her, was leaving the shop for the last time. She had not been able to buy any mourning, but Miss Mellins had sewed some crape on her old black mantle and bonnet, and having no gloves she slipped her bare hands under the folds of the mantle.

It was a beautiful morning, and the air was full of a warm sunshine that had coaxed open nearly every window in the street, and summoned to the window-sills the sickly plants nurtured indoors in winter. Ann Eliza's way lay westward, toward Broadway; but at the corner she paused and looked back down the familiar length of the street. Her eyes rested a moment on the blotched "Bunner Sisters" above the empty window of the shop; then they travelled on to the overflowing foliage of the Square, above which was the church tower with the dial that had marked the hours for the sisters before Ann Eliza had bought the nickel clock. She looked at it all as though it had been the scene of some unknown life, of which the vague report had reached her: she felt for herself the only remote pity that busy people accord to the misfortunes which come to them by hearsay.

She walked to Broadway and down to the office of the house-agent to whom she had entrusted the sub-letting of the shop. She left the key with one of his clerks, who took it from her as if it had been any one of a thousand others, and remarked that the weather looked as if spring was really coming; then she turned and began to move up the great thoroughfare, which was just beginning to wake to its multitudinous activities.

She walked less rapidly now, studying each shop window as she passed, but not with the desultory eye of enjoyment: the watchful fixity of her gaze overlooked everything but the object of its quest. At length she stopped before a small window wedged between two mammoth buildings, and displaying, behind its shining plate-glass festooned with muslin, a varied assortment of sofa-cushions, tea-cloths, pen-wipers, painted calendars and other specimens of feminine industry. In a corner of the window she had read, on a slip of paper pasted against the pane: "Wanted, a Saleslady," and after studying the display of fancy articles beneath it, she gave her mantle a twitch, straightened her shoulders and went in.

Behind a counter crowded with pin-cushions, watch-holders and other needlework trifles, a plump young woman with smooth hair sat sewing bows of ribbon on a scrap basket. The little shop was about the size of the one on which Ann Eliza had just closed the door; and it looked as fresh and gay and thriving as she and Evelina had once dreamed of making Bunner Sisters. The friendly air of the place made her pluck up courage to speak.

"Saleslady? Yes, we do want one. Have you any one to recommend?" the young woman asked, not unkindly.

Ann Eliza hesitated, disconcerted by the unexpected question; and the other, cocking her head on one side to study the effect of the bow she had just sewed on the basket, continued: "We can't afford more than thirty dollars a month, but the work is light. She would be expected to do a little fancy sewing between times. We want a bright girl: stylish, and pleasant manners. You know what I mean. Not over thirty, anyhow; and nice-looking. Will you write down the name?"

Ann Eliza looked at her confusedly. She opened her lips to explain, and then, without speaking, turned toward the crisply-curtained door.

"Ain't you going to leave the AD-dress?" the young woman called out after her. Ann Eliza went out into the thronged street. The great city, under the fair spring sky, seemed to throb with the stir of innumerable beginnings. She walked on, looking for another shop window with a sign in it.

The extraordinary American writer Edith Wharton was born Edith Newbold Jones on January 24th, 1862 to George Frederic Jones and Lucretia Stevens Rhinelander at their brownstone at 14 West Twenty-third Street in New York City. Her parents already had two older sons, Frederic Rhinelander, and Henry Edward.

Edith was baptized April 20, 1862, Easter Sunday, at Grace Church. To her friends and family she was apparently known as "Pussy Jones".

The 1860's were a time of Civil War in America but by the time Edith was three the war was over and a more normal life among Americans could resume.

From 1866 to 1872, the Jones family visited France, Italy, Germany, and Spain and Edith became fluent in French, German, and Italian. She was taught by a succession of tutors and governesses. Her thirst for learning was apparent at even this early age. So too was a streak of rebelliousness as she pushed back at society's standards of fashion and etiquette that were thought to be needed to help these young women marry well and to be displayed at balls and parties. She thought this superficial and oppressive.

Although he mother forbade her to read novels until she married (Edith it seems complied with that instruction) she read from her father's library and that of friends.

Edith first step to becoming a writer was inventing stories when she was around six. She would walk around the living room holding a book and reciting her story.

In 1872 at age ten, Edith was taken ill with typhoid fever while the family was at a spa in the Black Forest. The family returned to the United States that same year to begin a cycle of winters in New York and their summers in Newport, Rhode Island.

The following year, 1873, Edith wrote a short story and gave it to her mother to read. It was heavily criticised and Edith retreated to writing only poetry. Despite a child's need for a mother's approval and love, it was rare that she received either. This core relationship was indeed a troubled one.

By the time Edith was 15 she had translated a German poem "Was die Steine Erzählen" ("What the Stones Tell") by Heinrich Karl Brugsch, for which she was paid $50.

However her family did not wish to see her name in print (upper class women of the time only appeared in print to announce birth, marriage, and death). Consequently, the poem was published under the name of a friend's father, E. A. Washburn, a cousin of Ralph Waldo Emerson and a supporter of women's education and a great encourager of Edith's talents.

That same year, 1877, Edith had also secretly written a 30,000 word novella "Fast and Loose". Her central themes came from her experiences with her parents. She was very critical of her own work and would even write public reviews criticizing it. The following year, 1878, her father arranged for a collection of two dozen original poems and five translations, Verses, to be privately published.

In 1880 she had five poems published anonymously in the Atlantic Monthly, a much revered literary magazine. Despite these early successes, she was not encouraged to publish by others but did continue to write.

Edith was courted by Henry Stevens from 1880 and after two years they became engaged. A month before their marriage the engagement abruptly ended.

In 1885, at age 23, she married Edward (Teddy) Robbins Wharton, who was 12 years her senior. He was from a well-established Boston family, a sportsman and a gentleman of the same social class and shared her love of travel.

However this desirable match was blighted. From the late 1880s until 1902, he suffered acute depression. At that latter time his depression manifested as a more serious disorder, after which they lived almost exclusively at their estate; The Mount.

In October 1889 her poem "The Last Giustiniani", was published in Scribner's Magazine.

At age 29 Edith finally had her first short story published. "Mrs. Manstey's View." It had very little success, and another year was to elapse until she published again.

She completed "The Fullness of Life" following her annual European trip with Teddy. Burlingame was critical of this story but Wharton did not want to make edits to it. This story, along with many others, speaks about her marriage. She sent Bunner Sisters to Scribner's in 1892. The editor in chief, Edward L Burlingame wrote back that it was too long for Scribner's to publish. This story is believed to be based on an experience she had as a child. It did not see publication until 1916.

After a visit with her friend, Paul Bourget, she wrote "The Good May Come" and "The Lamp of Psyche". "The Lamp of Psyche" was a comical story with verbal wit and sorrow. After "Something Exquisite" was rejected by Burlingame, she lost confidence in herself.

By 1894 she had decided to write about her travels. This allied with her other interests of garden and interior design came to a publishing point in 1897 with a co-authorship on The Decoration of Houses, the first of several design books.

Her thirst for travel and to explore eventually meant some sixty trips across the Atlantic to travel across Europe and even Morocco.

Her husband, Edward, shared this love of travel and for years they would spend four, or more, month abroad until his illness deteriorated their quality of life such that they remained in America.

In 1888, the Wharton's and their friend, James Van Alen, took a cruise through the Aegean islands. Wharton was 26. The trip cost a substantial amount: $10,000 and lasted four months. Edith kept a travel journal during this trip that was later published as The Cruise of the Vanadis, her earliest known travel writing.

In 1901, Wharton wrote a two act play called "Man of Genius". This play was about an English man who was having an affair with his secretary. The play was rehearsed, but was never produced. One of her earliest literary endeavors (1902) was the translation of the play, "Es Lebe das Leben" ("The Joy of Living"), by Hermann Sudermann. "The Joy of Living" was a short lived Broadway production but was, however, a successful book.

She collaborated with Marie Tempest to write another play, but the two only completed four acts before Marie decided she was no longer interested in costume plays.

In 1902, she designed The Mount, her estate in Lenox, Massachusetts. Edith wrote several of her novels there, including The House of Mirth (1905), the first of many chronicles of life in old New York. At The Mount, she entertained the cream of American literary society, including her close friend, novelist Henry James, who described the estate as "a delicate French chateau mirrored in a Massachusetts pond".

Although she spent many months traveling The Mount was her primary residence until 1911.

With her marriage falling apart, due mainly to Edward's illness, she decided to move to Paris, living first at 53 Rue de Varenne, Paris, in an apartment that belonged to George Washington Vanderbilt II.

In 1908 her husband's mental state was determined to be incurable. In the same year, she began an affair with Morton Fullerton, a journalist for The Times, in whom she also found an intellectual partner.

She divorced Edward Wharton in 1913 after 28 years of marriage.

In 1914 Edith was preparing for her summer vacation when World War I broke out. Many fled Paris, but she moved back to her Paris apartment on the Rue de Varenne and for the next four years was a tireless, ardent supporter of the French war effort.

In August 1914 at the onset of War she opened a workroom for unemployed women; here they were fed and paid one franc a day. Thirty women started and this soon doubled to sixty, and their sewing business began to thrive. When the Germans invaded Belgium in the fall of 1914 and Paris was flooded with Belgian refugees, she helped to set up the American Hostels for Refugees, which gave shelter, meals, clothes and then an agency to help them find work. She raised and collected more than $100,000 on their behalf.

In early 1915 she organized the Children of Flanders Rescue Committee, which gave shelter to almost 900 Belgian refugees whose homes had been bombed by the Germans.

Aided by her influential connections in the French government, she and her long-time friend Walter Berry (then president of the American Chamber of Commerce in Paris), were among the few foreigners in France allowed to travel to the front lines. She and Berry made a total of five journeys between February and August 1915, which Edith described in a series of articles that were first published in Scribner's Magazine and later as Fighting France: From Dunkerque to Belfort, which became a bestseller. Travelling by car, they drove through the war zone; one decimated French village after another. She visited the trenches that were within earshot of artillery fire. She wrote, "We woke to a noise of guns closer and more incessant...and when we went out into the streets it seemed as if, overnight, a new army had sprung out of the ground".

During the war years Edith worked tirelessly in charitable efforts for refugees, the injured, the unemployed, and the displaced.

On 18 April 1916, the President of France appointed her Chevalier of the Legion of Honour, the country's highest award, in recognition of her dedication to the war effort.

Edith also kept up her own work during the war, which was now a prodigious output of novels, short stories, and poems, as well as reporting for the New York Times and keeping up her enormous correspondence. She urged Americans to support the war effort and to enter the war with its enormous resources of industry and men. She wrote the popular romantic novel Summer in 1916, the war novella, The Marne, in 1918, and A Son at the Front in 1919, (though not published until 1923).

When the war ended, she watched the Victory Parade from the Champs Elysees' balcony of a friend's apartment. After four years of intense effort, she decided to leave Paris in favor of the peace and quiet of the countryside. She settled a few miles north of Paris in Saint-Brice-sous-Forêt, buying an eighteenth-century house on seven acres of land which she called Pavillon Colombe. Edith would live there in summer and autumn for the rest of her life. She spent winters and springs on the French Riviera at Sainte Claire du Vieux Chateau in Hyeres.

Edith was a committed supporter of French imperialism, describing herself as a "rabid imperialist", and the war solidified her political views. After the war she travelled to Morocco as the guest of Resident General Hubert Lyautey and wrote a book, In Morocco, about her experiences. Wharton's writing on her Moroccan travels is full of praise for the French administration and for Lyautey and his wife in particular.

During the post war years she divided her time between Hyères and Provence, where she finished The Age of Innocence in 1920, which won the 1921 Pulitzer Prize for literature, making Edith the first woman to win the award.

Edith returned to the United States only once after the war, receiving an honorary doctorate degree from Yale University in 1923.

Edith included in her intellectual circle many of the great artists of her day; Henry James, Sinclair Lewis and Jean Cocteau were among her guests at the time. Theodore Roosevelt and Kenneth Clark were also friends. Of particular note was her meeting with F. Scott Fitzgerald, described as "one of the better known failed encounters in the American literary annals".

In 1934 Edith's autobiography A Backward Glance was published. This glossed over much of the problems in her life barely registering the criticism of her mother, her difficulties with Teddy, and her affair with Morton Fullerton.

On June 1, 1937 Wharton was at the French country home of Ogden Codman, working on a revised edition of The Decoration of Houses, when she suffered a heart attack and collapsed.

Edith Wharton died of a stroke some months later on August 11, 1937 at Le Pavillon Colombe, her 18th-century house on Rue de Montmorency in Saint-Brice-sous-Forêt at 5:30 pm. At her bedside was her friend, Mrs. Royal Tyler. The street is today called rue Edith Wharton.

Edith was buried at the Cimetière des Gonards in Versailles, "with all the honors owed a war hero and a chevalier of the Legion of Honor....a group of a hundred friends sang a verse of the hymn "O Paradise"...." She is buried next to her long-time friend, Walter Berry.

French Ways and Their Meaning, 1919
In Morocco, 1920
The Writing of Fiction, 1925
A Backward Glance, 1934

The Book of the Homeless, 1916

CINEMA
The House of Mirth (La Maison du Brouillard), a 1918 silent film adaptation (6 reels).
The Glimpses Of The Moon, a 1923 silent film adaptation (7 reels)
The Age of Innocence, a 1924 silent film adaptation (7 reels) (of the 1920 novel)
The Marriage Playground, a 1929 film adaptation (70 minutes) (of the 1928 novel The Children)
 The Age of Innocence, a 1934 film adaptation (9 reels).
Strange Wives, a 1935 film adaptation (8 reels) (of the 1934 short story Bread Upon the Waters)
The Old Maid, a 1939 film adaptation (95 minutes) (of the 1924 short novella)
Ethan Frome (99 minutes) directed by John Madden. 1993,
The Age of Innocence (138 minutes) directed by Martin Scorsese. 1993,
The Reef (88 minutes) directed by Robert Allan Ackerman. 1999.
The House of Mirth (140 minutes) directed by Terence Davies. 2000.

TV
Ethan Frome, a 1960 (CBS) TV US adaptation.
Looking Back, a 1981 TV US adaptation of two biographies of Edith Wharton.
The House of Mirth, a 1981 TV US adaptation.
The Buccaneers, a 1995 BBC mini-series, starring Carla Gugino and Greg Wise.

THEATRE
The Man of Genius in 1901
"Es Lebe das Leben" ("The Joy of Living"), by Hermann Sudermann in 1902 - Translator.
The House of Mirth was adapted as a play in 1906.
The Age of Innocence was adapted as a play in 1928.

www.ingramcontent.com/pod-product-compliance
Lightning Source LLC
Chambersburg PA
CBHW071410170626
46811CB00003B/1334